Pray For Hell

Supernatural Sampson County
(Book 2)

MORRIGAN AUSTIN

PRAY FOR HELL
by
Morrigan Austin
Copyright © Morrigan Austin 2011
Edited by Jennii Peterschick
Cover Copyright © Ravenswood Publishing 2018
Published by Dark Serpent
(An Imprint of Ravenswood Publishing)

DARK SERPENT

Ravenswood Publishing
1275 Baptist Chapel Rd.
Autryville, NC 28318
http://www.ravenswoodpublishing.com

Printed in the U.S.A.

ISBN-13: 978-0692360842
ISBN-10: 0692360840

For Amber Rendon, great writing partner, dear friend and lover of this story. I hope I made you proud.

To Jennii Peterschick my editor and best friend, thank you for keeping my evil side alive and kicking.

PROLOGUE
(MISSY & JUNO)

Missy had almost waited too long to leave her hiding spot in the woods, the thunder sounded like the sharp report of gunfire from the east and she flinched as though she could feel shrapnel penetrate her skin. For an hour now she'd been trying to sleep, but between the thunder in the distance and the shrill shrieks of laughter coming from her mother's room she was unable to find the peace she needed to help her drift off. Finally, she rose and began the laborious task of pushing her bed to the other side of the room just as the clouds burst open and the first few drops of rain began. Dropping back down on her bed she listened with bated breath, waiting for the water to start its slow drip upon the floor where her bed had just been. Maybe the sound would be the needed antidote to her insomnia.

Missy Jackson wasn't an ugly girl, though it seemed she tried too hard to hide the ugliness she felt inside as well as out. At the painful age of thirteen she'd began to dye her bright red hair, often in rainbow hues that could not be bought at the local beauty supply stores. Instead, she figured out that packs of 'Kool-Aid' worked just as well and were far cheaper at only ten cents each. Her current color of choice was 'wild cherry' which almost made her hair look pink in the right light. She had vibrant hazel eyes that seemed to stare right through you; her mother often said her mouth was heart-shaped like Bernadette Peters, which led Missy to believe she had a Kewpie Doll's face. In her opinion it wasn't that flattering a thought. Her father had left a long time ago when Missy was only two and she lived in a half dilapidated, five room mobile home just on the edge of town. She'd realized from the first day of school at Midway High that she'd never be head cheerleader or homecoming queen.

The thunder came again and as if to punctuate the sound of her mother's witchy screech from across the hall. Groaning she tugged the pillow from beneath her head and brought it over her face, curling it around to cover both ears. She half-heartedly hoped she'd succeed in suffocating herself and end her teenage suffering once and for all. At the age of seventeen she'd already endured most of her high school years, and often times wished her mother had done the right thing when she'd been born. She felt she should have been put in a burlap sack, weighted down with cement bricks and tossed into William's Lake like some unwanted puppy. After all, her mother was nothing more than a bitch in heat it seemed, dragging up every man she could find that would give her the time of day. This new one was no different, she'd met him in the Red Dog Saloon about two days ago, that meant his welcome was almost worn out and he'd soon decide he'd had enough, either that or her mother would grow bored with her new toy and move on to the next.

In pseudo silence she waited until she was at the point where air was almost completely depleted before she slowly brought the pillow up and turned her head to look over and up at the leak in her ceilin. She could see the iridescent illumination of each drop when the lightning flashed and had just enough time to watch its descent before it disappeared again into the darkness. It wasn't long before she felt hypnotized and her eyelids grew heavy, it seemed there was no other sound at all, and then... *he* was there. Jerked from her reverie, she struggled to sit upright on the bed and twisted her entire body until she was sitting Indian style upon the covers waiting for the next lightning strike to be sure she wasn't seeing things. It came, and as it did the figure she saw lifted his head to gaze at her with amusement in his eyes and a jarring smile upon his lips. She had not heard him enter, there was no way he could have gotten in without her door making the usual squeaking noise upon hinges that had not been oiled in far too many years to count.

Fear as thick as mud ran through her veins and her adrenaline kicked in as she stood quickly and began to fumble with a dresser drawer to find a flashlight. Once again her mother had failed to pay the electric bill on her meager earnings working at the saloon. About the time her hand closed upon the stem of her flashlight and her thumb found the button, she felt strong arms go around her and a warm breath upon her ear. "Shhh... don't make a sound now, I'm not here to hurt ya." Missy

3

closed her eyes; the voice was like velvet and had a slight twang to it. She hadn't even seen his face good enough to know what he looked like, but she could tell that no one could own a voice like that and not have the looks to match. "Wh... who are you... what the hell do you want?" Her own voice shook as she spoke, but she had one arm pulled slightly forward and bent ready to land an elbow to his ribs if he said the wrong thing or made the wrong move. Though she may have been enjoying the feel of his arms embracing her a little too much she was not about to just give in and let him have his way with her if that's what he was after.

"I'm Jesse's brother... Juno." He paused and Missy shook her head feeling his lips brush against her temple. "Who the fuck is Jesse? I don't know a Jesse." Instantly she felt the release of his arms and he was laughing as he backed a few paces away. "Damn that's sad; you don't even know the names of the men your mommy brings home to fuck?" Anger rushed through her like a hot flame and she turned hurling the flashlight at the place she thought he might be standing. "Fuck you! Why the hell are you in my room? If you think I'm about to give you what my stupid cunt mother is giving your brother in there you're wrong! That's not me." Still shaking she lowered herself onto the edge of her bed but kept at the ready in case he came at her again. "Hell no... I was bored as hell sitting outside, then it started to rain I thought I'd come in and try and hurry him up. Looks like he's going to be at it all night though." There was a flare as he struck a match and lit a cigarette, then she heard footsteps and soon felt a weight pressing down upon the bed at her side. Glancing over about the time another streak lit the sky she saw his face and felt her stomach turn a flip. Though the glimpse was fleeting she had been able to catch just enough to tell that he had black hair tinted with a hint of blue, his eyes were piercing, the blue of the sky on a cloudless summer day, and his skin was completely unmarred by even the slightest blemish. "Sorry, I just didn't hear you come in and..." Her words seemed to fall off into silence as she heard the flick of the match and smelled the smoke from his cigarette. Suddenly the craving hit her hard. "You got another one of those?"

Juno handed her the pack and his matches. "So what's up with the lights? I mean, I know there's a storm and all but I saw lights on in the house down the street." Missy lit up and took a long drag from the Marlboro handing the pack back to him. "Yeah, my mom didn't pay the bill again." Juno shook his head and laughed. "So you must be Missy Sue... your mom mentioned you when we came in tonight." She was up and in motion then, pacing across the floor. "Don't call me that, only she calls me that and I fucking hate it." He held up his hands as though warding off her anger. "Sorry, sorry, what you wanna be called then?" Turning to face him she stared hard where she assumed he still sat and spoke in a rush, "Missy... just Missy." For a long moment there was an awkward silence that hung between them like some heavy blanket, then Juno spoke up again and she could have sworn she saw his eyes light up, the color of a hot, coal; red, a sharp contrast from the pristine blue she had seen before. He reached into his jacket pocket and brought out a set of keys as the next streak of lightning lit up the sky. "I got the keys to Jesse's truck... wanna go for a ride... Missy?"

5

CHAPTER ONE
(THE FUNERAL)

The small group gathered beneath a dark and angry sky, collectively bearing an umbrella of sorrow for the man that had touched them both individually and as a pack. They were a family of friends brought together by a destiny that had been their communal cross to bear since birth. The dawn had marched dutifully across the land, conveying a somber gift of drizzle left over from last night's storm for the lost loved one. Somewhere along the horizon, the sun lazily climbed from bed and began its inevitable ascent in an effort to burn the incessant rain away. Bright and cheerful streaks of sunshine were subdued by a thick fog, which kindly screened the poignant party from those warm rays.

Presently no one said a word of the passing or of the obvious agony the deceased had suffered. His body had been mutilated. Muscles were shredded and bone snapped clean in half like twigs beneath the powerful bite of some half mad or crazed animal. For this reason they all shared one very common and uneasy reflection. By the law of breeding, Ashton Morris was due his father's position as pack alpha. Traditionally, a new alpha's reign was marked with celebration and joy but no such festivities were employed today. There was only anger and suspicion; both flamed to dizzying heights by Ashton's palpable absence among the pack. It was his duty to address them about his father's death and advise them on the suddenly uncertain future.

From most, he was given no additional sympathy for his personal and profound loss, which was unique to him alone. The majority, afforded him only blame and debt, both increasing tenfold with each silent minute that passed without an appearance. A simple symphony was conducted by nature. Birds called and leaves were rustled underfoot. Silent prayers gave way to final goodbyes before the fragile peace was broken. In the distance a noise echoed, both ominous and wretched as the wind elevated its tone. Ashton Morris howled long and low. Whether out of grief or triumph, no one among the pack could be positively sure.

The sound ended abruptly and in his mind, it was tethered by a mixture of sorrow and penance for what he'd done. He sat alone atop a hill shrouded with shrubbery, hidden except to those few whose keen eyes cut through the brush to see him there. His blood-tinged maw still hung slightly open as he panted in an effort to cool his burning body. He could not bring himself to be among them, nor could he have told them the truth of how his father had come to his end. His lungs ached with each breath he took and his ribs still felt as though they were struggling to break through his skin. He had to rest, he was sure the marks would be there for a few days and he'd have to stay away until they healed where no evidence of the fight would be left for prying eyes to see. Only three turned to see him as the mournful sound ended, his aunt, his grandfather, and his sister... Sera.

His gaze caught his sister's for a long moment, the eyes of the wolf mirroring those that were supremely human, before he turned away to break through the brush and find a place to lie down. Realization came with a sudden gust of fall wind and he snuffed the ground beginning to dig a hole for added warmth. He couldn't stay gone for long; in truth even a few days would be too much. He'd had a responsibility even before his father's death, and that responsibility was his younger sibling. Even though Sera had loved him, their father had become more and more enthralled with his secret life and less interested in raising his children. When Ashton had found out what he'd been doing with all his time, he'd seen no other way to save the pack but to finish it once and for all. Would they ever understand? None of them knew David Morris like his son did, there was not a single one that could see the truth behind those eyes that were adept at hiding everything.

The fact was, David Morris, had always been more concerned with making a fast buck than he had with the welfare of the pack. For years now he'd had a profound gambling problem that had caused him to begin abusing drugs as well as alcohol. There were so many times that Ashton had to divert Sera's attention from their father, unwilling to allow her view of him to be corrupted by the truth. Ashton cared about the pack, and though he'd done things he was not proud of, even though he'd acted out time and again in his teenage years... he was grown now. Ashton Morris was a man at twenty-four years of age. Still... there was a part of him that didn't think he was ready for all of... *this*. He wasn't at all sure that he'd be able to lead; the only thing he knew for sure was that he'd done the only thing he could to insure the safety of his family.

He'd wait, at least until they buried him. It was the way of the Morris family to bury their own and no one in the small town of Sampson County, North Carolina begrudged them their privacy. It didn't really seem odd that they were so close, as many of the farming families in the area were much the same. For over thirty-eight years now they had owned and farmed the land known as the Morris Ranch, they produced their own food as well as sold to markets to make a living. They bred horses, cattle, chickens, and pigs and grew some of the best crops for miles around. It wasn't the running of the farm that Ashton was worried about, as he'd been doing most of the work since he was old enough to drive a tractor at only twelve... it was taking over his father's place as alpha of the pack that bothered him most. Almost all of his family thought him too young and inexperienced to lead, and though he'd readily have given the opportunity over to his uncle, he knew the man wouldn't take it if for no other reason than respect for his brother. Ashton's worst fear was that they'd accuse him of murdering his father out of ambition. He finished digging his hole, paws now dirty with silt. Huffing loudly he settled in, the multiple hues of his coat melding in with the terrain, and closed his eyes preparing to spend the next few hours in a mixture of mourning and healing.

CHAPTER TWO
(THE POLICE STATION)

There was something strange happening in Sampson County. It was very clear to Jacy, from the moment she had first arrived in the small country town, that the residents of Sampson County, North Carolina were protective of their home. There was a sense of camaraderie in the air, thick and secretive, as though the wings of a huge raven spread over the rustic town and its inhabitant's intent on keeping prying eyes at bay. Nothing at all like New York, which was blatant and loud, busy and laced with a palpable sense of insanity.

Even now, almost a year after she had made the sojourn from NYC, Jacy still endured fleeting moments of culture shock. In fact, she was sure her face conveyed some of the surprise that usually accompanied those moments, as she stared, gaping, at her boss. "Did you just say... "The Spivey's Corner Cow Pageant?" she asked momentarily stunned. "It's a long standin' tradition in Sampson County, Crittenden. We get folk from as far as Polk County coming down to visit, and I reckon it's a fine way for the locals to become familiar with you." Sheriff Dalton drawled, scrutinizing her over the toothpick he thoughtfully chewed. "'Sides, you ain't got nothin' to worry about, Deputy. Wayne's gonna be there too."

"Well that's reassuring," Jacy muttered, cutting Wayne a sharp glance from the corner of her eye. He was busily reclining in the weathered chair at his desk, cradling the phone to his ear as he blustered importantly into the receiver. "Today?" Wayne glanced up from the paper he was currently running stubby fingers over to catch the glare Jacy sent his way. A slow grin began to crawl over his lips and he winked at her. Was this perhaps his idea? It had been a long time since Wayne had seen anything that looked closer to a possible affair and he was determined he'd have Jacy in his bed before the month was out.

It seemed something caught his attention though and he immediately renewed his interest in the business end of the phone that was glued to his ear. "How did he die? Mhmmm... I see. Well tell Ashton I'll be down there in the next hour or so." The finality of the dial tone as the person on the other end hung up sent a shiver down his spine. He hated this, but Dalton had made it his priority to take care of the Morris's 'problems' as it seemed the Sheriff was reluctant to do so himself. Wayne liked Ashton Morris, as a matter of fact the two were somewhat chummy but for some reason the farm gave him the creeps. He stood in one swift motion and started to shrug on his jacket as he spoke to Dalton, completely overlooking Jacy. "David Morris was found dead a few days ago. That was Clarice on the phone, she said they've already buried him, but there's talk that it was a murder. I think I'll go over there... talk to Ashton and find out what's going on."

Wayne might as well have been transparent, considering how easily his features shifted to convey his eager appreciation when he caught Jacy's glance. She barely contained the snort that wrinkled her nose as her gaze returned to Dalton. Arranging her mouth into a coaxing, sly, smile, the deputy leaned her hip back against the desk before vigorously pursuing the topic of the Spivey's Corner Cow Pageant. She was prepared to use every feminine trick in her arsenal to secure herself more responsibility and credible assignments. "Now Sheriff..." she began, only to be immediately silenced as Wayne discarded the phone into its cradle and announced the murder. Instantly straightening, Jacy pushed herself upright and stalked the short distance toward her desk, where her own jacket had been tossed on the back of her chair.

"A few days ago?" She interrupted, shoving one arm into the leather bomber. "Wait, they are only just now reporting this?" She asked, her tone ringing with unsuppressed shock. She wondered briefly, as she quickly jetted over toward Wayne, why the two men seemed nonchalant about an unreported death but knew better than to argue the point just then. "Give me those." She demanded, swooping beneath Wayne's outstretched arm to try and pluck the keys to his cruiser from his desk, nearly toppling over his cold coffee in her haste.

"Oh no you don't, don't go thinking that you're going to get involved in some murder or homicide just because you're from New York. Things like that just don't happen often here in Sampson County so you may as well stay here. I'm sure that Clarice is just running off at the mouth again. Mr. Morris likely passed in a very reasonable way... more like a heart attack of something with the way he worked that farm." Wayne scooped the keys out of her reach and into his beefy hand before she could grab them, cursing as the upset cup of coffee nearly spilled on his paperwork for the day. "Look Jacy... this isn't New York honey, I'll go down there, speak with Ashton and get this whole mess straightened out." He smirked as he turned to head to the door. "Besides, you need to make yourself presentable to deal with all those cows at the pageant, can't let a bunch of bovine mammals outshine ya now." He glanced at Dalton, the sheriff not looking as though he was quite as sure as Wayne that things were so easily explained away. "I'll be back in an hour or so, I'll take the walky in case you need me.

Jacy bristled, a scowl forming on her lips. "The hell I don't, and what have I told you about calling me honey." She gritted through her teeth as he neatly plucked the keys from her grasp. "Heart attack or not, don't you think it's weird? They kept a body for several days, deputy." Jacy continued stubbornly as she pivoted on her heel and marched toward the exit, sending Dalton a careless wave. "Besides, 'I reckon it's a fine way for the locals to become more familiar with me.'" She mimicked over her shoulder, pausing at the threshold with the door propped open against her hip. "The only competition the pageant has to worry about, Wayne is your stench. Let's hope, for your sake, that we don't have a repeat of the Miss Sampson County Pumpkin

Parade debacle on our hands." Without missing a beat, and without allowing her associate enough time to catch the door, Jacy strode purposely outside in the direction of the beat-up Jeep cruiser. "Don't forget to bring a change of clothes, just in case!" She yelled, before climbing inside his vehicle.

"Son of a..." He watched her walk toward the door and then glanced at Dalton who seemed to have a look that was a cross between mild worry and amusement on his face. "Take her with you Wayne; she needs to get to know the Morris' anyway." There was meaning behind his words but he clipped the sentence off with a brush of a large hand over his face and moved to settle down at his own desk. "Wayne?" The deputy turned around to face him again expectantly. "Be careful out there. Make sure you let Ashton know that we don't mean to pry, it's just routine." Wayne nodded and felt that shiver again as he exited and followed Jacy's trail. "I'm driving." He purposely failed to retaliate when she had mentioned the Pumpkin Parade as he'd ended up making quite an ass of himself having gotten exceedingly intoxicated during the festivities. Climbing into the driver's seat he buckled up and started the engine. Glancing over at her as she joined him he gave her a meaningful look. "Let me do the talking... you don't know these people like I do and trust me, they're a private lot. They've never been trouble and as long as you keep your big city mouth shut I'm sure things will be just fine." He began to back out of the parking space turning the jeep around, heading out to the highway.

CHAPTER THREE
(THE POLICE STATION)

Jacy was thankful that most of the drive to the Morris farm was made in silence. There had been one unpleasant moment, when the pair of deputies nearly came to blows over the radio. It was a short-lived tension, however, as Jacy had finally relented control to the man at her side. If there was one thing about Wayne that irked her more than anything else, it was the constant air of authority that surrounded him. She could handle her fair share of orders, and understood her place even if she didn't outwardly appear to be very accepting of it. She was the low 'woman' on the totem pole at the station, but there were some things she would never do for her boss or coworkers. "Next time your wife calls me at three in the morning looking for your ass, I'm going to give her Nancy's number." She muttered the half-hearted threat to Wayne as he expertly guided the Jeep onto a dusty back road, away from the main highway. She had only been out this far a handful of times, as it seemed the sheriff preferred to take care of the farmers himself. "Tell me about these people, Wayne. What are they like?" She asked, effectively cutting in before he could respond about his wife as she leaned forward and braced an elbow against the dashboard. Squinting at him through narrowed eyes, Jacy reached for the small notebook in her back pocket. It was a habit she had picked up in New York, keeping her own records, recording events in minute detail. Notebook in hand, she settled back against the faded leather of the seats and flipped the pad open with a flick of the wrist. "What should I expect?"

Wayne opened his mouth to reply but quickly shut it as she moved on ahead to the topic of the Morris'. He and Nancy Perkins had been having an affair now for over three years and if his wife ever found out... well there was his boy to think about. Even though Jameson was almost out of high school it would still be a hell of a bad situation for the kid. He glanced over at her as she jerked the notepad from her back pocket, watching the way her breasts jutted forward with the rise of her hips and shook his head with a snort. "You sure you didn't work for the FBI instead of the police department? You got a lot to get use to around here honey."

He turned his gaze back to the road ahead; they had about a mile left before they'd make it to the dirt road that led to the Morris Farm. "The Morris' are a private people, the largest farming family here in Sampson County. They stay to themselves mostly and usually only come to town to sell their crops when the harvest season comes around. Except the son, Ashton he comes into town quite a bit, mostly hanging out at the Red Dog

Saloon. But he's never been known to do much but sit and drink... been in a few bar fights but nothing real bad. He's young, mid-twenties or so. Got most of the women in these parts just salivating over him, but he shows no interest. I think he's gay myself but that's just my opinion." Of course he knew Ashton wasn't gay, nowhere near it but it helped his ego to say so. "He has a little sister, Sera Morris; she goes to school at Midway High. Straight 'A' student, good kid. The family lives on that farm and works it almost like it's some kind of commune. Just the grandpa, Old Jumper, David Morris, the dad... of course deceased now, an uncle... aunt... and there was the mother but she up and ran off from what we know. Suppose she got tired of farm living. As I said before they're quiet folk and we don't get into their business as long as things seem legit. I swear if I didn't know better I'd think they were either Mormon's or Amish." He paused as he maneuvered the jeep onto the dirt road and slowed a little to keep the hunk of metal from vibrating to the point of falling apart.

The entire time he spoke, Jacy had been scribbling across the blank paper, only pausing when Wayne drove over a particularly rough patch of road. Her hand wavered momentarily, as he commented on the younger Morris' sexual orientation. It was just like him to assume a man was gay if he wasn't publicly sleeping with half the town, or cheating on his wife, like him. She almost let a scorching retort roll off her tongue, but remembered quickly that she had almost ended up sleeping with the deputy herself, after a particularly wild night at the saloon. It said a lot about Sampson County's population and the male selection therein, if Wayne was getting action left and right. Besides the spare tire he carried nestled over the band of his pants, Jacy suspected the man was nearly bald, a fact she hadn't been able to confirm since he kept his cowboy hat religiously perched atop his pate. "Well, the kid should be out of school now. Maybe, if we're lucky, we can interview the whole family. Imagine that, deputy, just like those real cops on TV." Jacy smirked, flipping another page before jotting down a few questions that came to mind.

They went around a turn and the house suddenly became visible, a rather large Victorian style, whitewashed monstrosity. He glanced briefly over at her and sneered. "Yeah... imagine that." He shook his head concentrating on the drive and pulled the jeep to a stop just in front of a huge barn. "We're here to pay our condolences and make sure there was no foul play... nothing more. If Ashton says that everything is fine.. then everything IS fine. Got it?" He pulled the keys from the ignition, slid them into his jacket pocket and then opened his door. His left hand rose to position the hat more squarely on his head... and yes he was bald under there, then without waiting for Jacy he headed toward the house. Once up the steps he crossed the short distance of the porch and gave a loud knock on the screen door. "Mr. Morris? Clarice? Anyone home?" He glanced back a second to make sure Jacy was close and as he turned back he nearly jumped out of his skin. He hadn't heard any movement but there he was, Ashton Morris, sporting a black eye and a few scratches on one cheek that looked like they'd been pretty deep when they'd first happened. "Hey Ashton, can we come in?" Ashton didn't look as if he was too interested in letting the deputies in, but he merely nodded and opened the screen door stepping back to allow them both entry. "Everything alright Wayne?" Ashton's voice was smooth yet deep and resonate as he asked the ominous question that would surely lead to a detailed report of what had happened to his daddy. The deputy stepped in and turned to face the man again. "Well that depends, I got a call, from Clarice, saying that your daddy passed. What happened?"

Jacy couldn't shake the uncomfortable suspicion that Wayne was feeding her a lot of half-truths where the Morris' were concerned. Although he had been forthcoming, his information seemed almost selective, as though he was only telling her enough to keep her quiet. The thought didn't sit well with her, she hadn't yet become accustomed to walking the line both he and Dalton drew for her. Forced to employ a slow saunter behind Wayne's swaggering gait, she checked the urge to shove him out of her way. Coming to pause at the base of the steps, Jacy peered over the deputy's shoulder, her large brown eyes raking every avenue of their immediate surroundings, surroundings that were quickly overshadowed by Ashton Morris. Jacy, who had been expecting a young punk, was taken aback by Ashton and his appearance. It had nothing to do with the beating he had recently taken, all of which couldn't disguise the sharp contours and rugged good looks that lurked beneath the bruises. He had light brown hair that grazed his shoulders, his eyes were a piercing green unlike any color she'd ever seen on a painter's palette and the way he looked at her even in passing made her stomach jump as though she was on the Pirate Ship at its highest peak at the State Fair. She inhaled a quick, jerky breath through her teeth as her gaze dipped over his shoulders, which were wide and solid beneath the cotton of his plaid shirt, lower still across the distinct definition of his chest. She dimly heard Wayne greet Ashton, and was aware that he had moved inside the dwelling, leaving her no choice but to follow. All Jacy could think of was how she had never seen a more fantastic pair of jeans, slung low over lean hips and faded from wear, she was suddenly glad her eyes were hidden by her sunglasses. Wayne cleared his throat forcefully, jerking her mind away from a round-trip tour of Mr. Ashton Morris. She said the first thing that came to mind. "Is it a common practice, here on the farm, to wait several days after a death before notifying the authorities?"

Several days' growth cast a shadow around the contours of his face, his hair was slightly mussed, the flannel was stretched taut across his upper body and yes those jeans were extremely old. He had started to answer Wayne when the female cut in and his deep green gaze paused at once upon her face. For what seemed like several seconds he held her there, pinned with the attentiveness of a predator before a smile broke over his lips. "She must be new." He and Wayne shared a small bit of humor that Ashton seemed far more at ease with than the deputy. "Heart attack... at least we think that's what done it. I found him in the south field; he'd been mowing the weed growth out there. Best I can tell he must have suffered a heart attack, fell off the mower, and the side blade caught him... well it was nasty. I'd rather not go into details and to answer your question... deputy," he paused for a brief moment waiting for a name that was never given, "yes, it is common practice, old practices die hard. Our family holds a wake for at least five days before we bury the earthly remains. Our dead are the families problem... not that of the local coroner, that's the way we like it. We're not too partial to autopsies, if you know what I mean."

Shoving both hands in his pockets he glanced at Wayne again and then back to Jacy. "We bury our own... we don't really care to get involved with the outside world where our dead are concerned." It almost seemed like a warning more than an explanation as he fixed her with those strange green eyes again. "You said Clarice called?" He was getting tired of that old biddy, sticking her nose in their business. He'd be sure that she'd be packed and out of there within the next few days. It was hard to find good help, but he was sure that Sera could deal with the cooking and cleaning until they could find a more trustworthy person to take on the household chores. Even though the farm housed the extended family, an aunt, an uncle, himself, Sera and their grandfather, there was too much work on the farm itself to take time for washing the clothes, cooking, and cleaning. "You ah... want a cup of coffee or something Wayne? Miss?" They hadn't been properly introduced yet and he was waiting for Wayne to do the honors. "Oh... Ashton, this is Jacy Crittenden, she's moved here from New York." Ashton couldn't help that this knowledge set his teeth on edge but he only smiled and nodded. "Ashton Morris, pleasure to meet you ma'am." His accent was sharp, not quite a southern drawl but still pleasant to the ears. He turned to head to the kitchen not concerned whether they'd follow. There was no end to the nosy people in this town, present company included.

Jacy barely contained the shiver that crawled over her flesh when Ashton aimed the potency of his startling gaze at her. Straightening her slender shoulders, she refused to fidget beneath his surveillance. Instead, she stared back at him and flashed what she hoped was a charming smile. Though he gave no outward behavior that appeared threatening, she clearly read the warning in his easily offered explanation. With some dismay, she realized that his eyes, which flashed violently as he spoke, had completely stripped her clean of authority... and for one brief second, she was reduced to the role of prey to predator. With her notepad still in hand, and the pen poised for action, Jacy merely listened and nodded during the small lapses of silence that fell between them. Internally, she berated her body and mind for responding to the physical appearance of Ashton Morris. It was the warm flush that spread across her flesh when he moved, causing those muscles to chord expectantly and the mild memory of his challenging gaze.

From the way his body was speaking to her, Jacy knew that Ashton Morris was hiding something and she was determined to get to the bottom of it with or without the station's support. "Sure, I'll have a cup." She said this snapping her notepad shut after hastily scribbling, her hands sunk deep into her pockets, a classic sign of concealment. "Big place you have here, Mr. Morris. Live here all your life?" she asked as she followed him and Wayne into the kitchen. "Nothing like my home." She continued as she watched him subtly. "Ever been to the city, Ashton? You don't mind if I call you Ashton, do you? New York? Nothing like Sampson County, you'd be amazed." She shrugged out of her jacket and tossed it across a kitchen chair before moving toward the counter, right next to him. "I like it strong... no cream or sugar... the coffee."

There was always a fresh pot brewing, it was commonplace on most farms and here little miss New York would find nothing strange. He chuckled softly as she came to stand beside him, making sure that he understood she was talking about the coffee, but as he turned to hand her a cup, strong and black just like she liked it, he could tell he'd had an effect on her, but just what kind of effect he wasn't completely sure. "Yes, I've lived here all my life, since the day I was born and the only time I've been out of Sampson County was once when the sausage packing machine went down and we had to take our hogs up to the slaughter house in Charlotte. Other than that I don't travel much." He winked in her direction his boots creating a hollow thud as he headed over to the table to take a seat where Wayne had already parked his carcass long before. Settling another cup down before the deputy he sat back and laced his broad hands together. "I always knew he'd go this way, hell, I guess we all did. You know how hard he worked here. He was still young of course but he did eat a lot of what we farmed. After a while all that greasy meat is bound to kill you." He didn't seem too shook up about his father's death and only he knew the metaphors he used meant nothing at all, but it could easily be explained away as acceptance. Ashton was stronger than a lot of his family gave him credit for. This was something they'd be sure and figure out soon enough. "I'm sorry Clarice bothered you Wayne, she's old, I think she reads way too much into a lot of things that go on here in Sampson County and she's always cooking up something to tell those women at the salon in town."

He glanced over at Jacy again and grabbed the chair next to him pulling it out for her. "You can sit you know... I don't bite, unless you bite first." He was starting to have a little fun flirting with the deputy and she wasn't hard on the eyes in the least. His gaze raked over her and he instantly felt his skin flush hot. She was short, around five four with black hair and eyes just a shade lighter. Her skin was lightly tanned, he could tell she didn't visit the salon often but he found that oddly refreshing. Most of the women in town were painted up too much, their hair always looked too nice. He had a desire for something far more natural, hence the reason he wasn't known to spend much time in their company. Reminding himself to keep it cool he looked away, waiting for Wayne's reply. "It's alright Ashton; I've known Clarice about as long as you have if not longer. I think she's going senile if you ask me. I'm real sorry to hear about your daddy though, he was a good man." Ashton nodded in agreement, though he couldn't completely feel the truth of the words given the circumstances. There was a lot that most outsiders had no idea about where David Morris was concerned.

Despite the raw, animal magnetism that Ashton exuded, Jacy was relieved by the noisy distraction overhead. Her attention was wrangled from the man of the house, and directed instead toward the opposite wall as she followed the muffled footsteps on the stairs. Canting her head, she stared toward the hallway that led to the living room area and finally removed her sunglasses settling them on the table before her. From the shadows a young woman stepped into view, her dark red hair trailing in her wake. She stumbled to a pause as she raised her gaze from the floor and observed the officers. Jacy fixed her lips in a warm smile; noticing, as she scrutinized the new arrival, that the girl couldn't be more than fifteen. "Hello, I'm deputy Crittenden." she said. Standing from the chair she'd seated herself in, Jacy approached the girl with her hand outstretched invitingly. She didn't miss the wary glance the youth shot first at her hand, or the way her slender brows furrowed in confusion. Jacy paused, barely daring to breathe as she waited for the young girl to respond. She felt the first pang of adrenaline kick in when the girl looked questioningly toward Ashton, as though seeking permission to proceed with the introduction Jacy had instigated.

CHAPTER FOUR
(THE MORRIS FARM)

"It's quite alright." Jacy continued, ignoring the men behind her. "We just came over, Wayne and I that is, to talk a little business with Mr. Morris and to pay our respects. We heard about your father's death." Jacy shifted from one foot to the other a tactic she employed to block Ashton from the young girl's view. This simple isolation forced the child to focus on Jacy, who was waiting with a warm smile. Her eyes flickered to the space between them when her hand was finally accepted and limply shaken. "Sera Morris." The girl said, finally offering a brief smile of her own. "Nice to meet you, Sera. Are you Ashton's daughter?" Jacy asked, releasing her firm grip on Sera's hand. "Daughter? No." Sera responded with a shake of her head, her smile widening as the endeavor became genuine. "He's my brother." Jacy looked slightly embarrassed. "Oh, I see. You both have the same lovely eyes." It was Sera's turn to blush at the compliment. "Thank you, Ms. Crittenden." Sera responded, wiping her palms down her thighs before ducking around Jacy. Jacy nodded, slowly pivoting to face the two men that had remained silent throughout the exchange. Her eyes strayed from Wayne to Ashton, and she felt, more than witnessed, the flamboyant confidence that radiated from his lounging figure.

This man, she thought, was the walking definition of trouble. It was intuition that blasted this base information into her sharp mind. The grin at her mouth faltered as her gaze connected with his, and though his expression remained open, Jacy detected the slightest trace of tension tightening his jaw. "I was just going to start dinner..." Sera said to her brother, pointing to the refrigerator as she passed his seat. Again, Jacy was struck by the acquiesce that was suggested in both Sera's manner of speech and actions toward her brother. She couldn't remember the last time she had seen such a respectful teenager. She wondered, her fingers itching to grab hold of her notebook, if Sera's behavior stemmed from affection or perhaps fear.

Jacy's assertion to keep their eyes from meeting would be a waste of energy. No eye contact was needed where the Morris's were concerned and Sera no doubt felt the press of his conscience within the fine webbing of her brain. It told her to show no fear, to keep calm and accept the woman's outstretched hand as she would have any ordinary visitor... of which they never had many. While the two made their acquaintance he found himself checking out the rear view and appreciating greatly what he saw. Wayne caught that open appreciation instantly and nudged Ashton with a good-natured grin curling the corners of his lips, showing tobacco stained teeth. A low chuckle ebbed from the depths of Ashton's throat and he was instantly reminded of how many nights he'd spent in the drunk tank of the jail with only Wayne for company. At times it was good to have friends on the force, if you could call the small police department a 'force' however Ashton seldom made a habit of getting into trouble at the Red Dog Saloon if he could help it.

As Sera brought up the subject of dinner, Ashton stood and walked over to her, an arm placed around her shoulders. What would likely strike Jacy more now than before was that the girl was just a foot shorter than her brother. It seemed they grew them tall and proud in the Morris family. "Don't worry about dinner, we're going out. You're grandpa's making good on that meal he owes you for your birthday last month." In fact he was sure Jumper would be along any minute now and this was as much a way of giving the deputies their chance to take their leave as it was a way of stopping Sera from fumbling in the cabinets for the few pots and pans they owned. Wayne grasped the top of his pants and belt hitching them up over his gut as he took the hint for what it was and stood from his place at the table.

"Well, we won't keep you Ashton, I'm sure you need to be heading out before too long if you plan to get a good seat wherever you decide to go." It was a Friday night and he knew there would be a line at both of the better restaurants in town. "We need to get on back anyway, come on Jacy." He turned toward the door with one last look at Sera. That girl was growing up to be the spitting image of her momma... Wayne missed the woman. Good looks and elegance even though she had been small town born and bred. When she'd gone missing there had been a lot of people in town that kicked up a fuss over it, speculations made, and long hours spent looking for any sign of her under the direction of David Morris, but she'd never been found and it was finally determined that she'd simply ran off with another man though Wayne couldn't understand that... she'd always seemed so dedicated to her family. Wayne was already at the door pushing open the screen and holding it for Jacy to make her exit. "I'll see ya around Ash... you take care now and if you need anything let me know. Momma will probably be over in a day or two with a cake, you know how she is, always making cakes when there's a death in town." Ashton smiled and nodded. "I'll be looking for her, Wayne. I do love your momma's chocolate cake." His gaze raked over Jacy again and he inwardly hoped he'd be seeing her soon... perhaps in a more comfortable situation than the one they were in now. "You take care deputy Crittenden; it was a real pleasure meeting you." That slow grin crawled over his lips again; the sharp contrast between his perfect white teeth and Wayne's stained ones was almost startling.

CHAPTER FIVE
(THE MORRIS FARM)

Sera moved with a feline grace, careful to keep enough distance between her and the deputies while remaining close enough to watch the pair depart. Once the engine of their police beater roared to life, the young girl turned her eyes toward her brother, making no attempt to conceal the uncertainty that swirled brightly in the dark depths. "What was that about, Ashton?" She asked in a tone the was dimly threaded with accusation. Her sibling; the wild and reckless Morris son, the one who made all the local women nuts. Sera had never understood why the girls in her class were forbidden to stay overnight by their parents. Something about her brother being a loose cannon, too dangerous. Not to mention the fact that her own family would never have allowed it anyway. *"Ashton?"* She'd ask incredulously. *"Not my brother, you've got him all wrong."* She had defended him to the end, against all grudges both foreign and domestic. But times had changed and it was written on her face, clear as a bright, cloudless day. Her comfort zone had been eroded; overrun with equal parts fear and mistrust, and violated by the grief of losing her dad.

"Wayne's never come by like that before. Not with a notepad in hand... well in his partner's hand." Granted, it hadn't been Wayne who was jotting down notes, but to the sixteen-year-old eye, it all looked the same. Instinctively, Sera crossed her arms over her chest and glanced away. She chewed on her bottom lip while she waited for him to answer, fighting back the surge of unanswered questions that flanked her mind. What really happened to dad? Had the same fate fell upon her mom? And why, most importantly, wasn't Ashton doing something about it?

Wayne situated his bulk into the seat and turned the engine over just as John "Jumper" Morris came out of the barn nearest the house. In his hands he carried what looked like two dead hens. His fingers were white knuckled with the grip he had around their legs and their heads flopped as though they would become detached at any moment. Wayne rolled down the window of the cruiser allowing the cool air that had just started to circulate to escape and called to the old man. "Looks like dinner!" He laughed slightly and glanced over at Jacy then back to Jumper. "Nah, takin' 'em to be cleaned and then frozen. I'll call ya when I get ready to cook 'em." With his free hand Jumper gave a mock salute to Wayne and a grin that showed teeth that did not go with the age he carried on his face. It was said that Jumper was close to seventy-five but he didn't look a day over fifty. His skin was tanned and lined perfectly

32

to give him the appearance of a cowboy from an old and well-loved western. His clothes were dusty, his hair a contrast of grays, blacks, and silvers that looked as though they'd been placed their on purpose. He was extremely handsome, even if his eyebrows were a bit bushy. "I'll take you up on that offer anytime." Wayne returned the gesture and revving up the engine he put the jeep in motion.

The corner of Jacy's mouth had curled downward even further as Wayne traded a greeting with the old man. For quite some time, she had been thinking that the community was trying to send her a message. Something like 'not welcome here, or go away.' Today, it had finally clicked into place. Standing in the Morris' kitchen, being talked over and talked around while the men took care of business. "That was a real shitty thing to do, Wayne." She said without cutting a glance in his direction. They were almost back to the station by now and she was so angry she could practically feel the adrenaline vibrating beneath her flesh, pulsing for release. Jacy wasn't the type that tried to fit into her surroundings, she never had been and never would be. But, for her sister's sake, she'd toned it down a bit. This was their fresh start, after all. This backwoods, bible-thumping, gossip riddled little community was there new beginning. "Don't shut me down like that again. I don't care what you say, or how buddy-buddy you and the Morris' are. You are either working with me or against me." She bit the words out through a tightly clenched jaw. Wayne glanced over at Jacy as they pulled into the station, after her diatribe he'd remained silent for the rest of the ride. Turning slightly in his seat he lifted his hand, pointing a finger straight at her. "Listen here girly, this is my town, my jurisdiction... I've been here longer than you, I grew up here. You are from another world and the way we do things here are not by New York standards. If you don't like it, you can always go peddling your high city ass back where you came from." As they pulled into the parking lot and without giving her a chance to respond he unbuckled his seat belt, opened his door then got out slamming it hard. He'd leave her there to think about his words and make a decision on her own. He liked Jacy, hell, he was beginning to like her a lot, but she was one filly in serious need of breaking.

CHAPTER SIX
(THE MORRIS FARM)

Back at the Morris Farm the tension had just gotten far worse than it had been while the deputies had been there. Ashton had returned back to the kitchen now and stood gazing out the window over the sink as Sera's voice cut firmly into his thoughts. For a moment he couldn't answer. "Nothing... it was about nothing." He wasn't sure he could even form the words that wouldn't surely plant suspicion in her mind. Wasn't she already suspicious enough? Turning he faced her and watched her for a long moment. Those arms laced tightly over her chest reminded him so much of their mother. She had that same stubborn set to her jaw and her eyes seemed to have become darker with an underlying accusation. He loved her so much; all he ever wanted to do was to keep her and the rest of the family safe there weren't many of them left.

With these thoughts causing his chest to swell he finally decided she was old enough that he couldn't keep everything from her forever. Exhaling he took a drag from his cigarette he'd lit just a moment before and walked to the table to put it out in the ashtray. He suddenly felt he couldn't look her directly in the eyes. "Clarice called the station and told Wayne about dad. She apparently made it sound as though there was foul play. They came to check it out." He knew what she was thinking then; he also knew what her next question would be before she even asked it. There had been foul play, their dad had been murdered... the only thing Sera didn't know and he prayed it wasn't even a thought in her mind, was that the one that had killed their father was right there unable to lift his gaze from the tabletop.

As Ashton exhaled, Sera watched the delicate rings of smoke waft through the air between them. She was close enough to see the tension cording the sinew at his broad shoulders, and understood that he was concealing truths and forming half-lies. While at the window, staring out over the vast and verdant farmland, Sera had been sure he was about to confess something to her. Her mind mentally prepared, erecting sky-high walls of self-preservation. She visibly tensed, as though suspended in mid-air, one short step away from the end of the tightrope she'd been balancing on so long. Then he evaded... and the breath left her lungs in one painful whoosh. The screen door creaked in protest as Jumper pushed into the kitchen, startling her. She swung around to face him, squeaking in surprise.

Almost comically Jumper stepped a half step backward and struck a defensive pose as Sera turned to face him when he came in the door. Chuckling quietly he moved to the table and lay the hens down before reaching to ruffle her hair. "Why so jumpy there little red?" He'd called her mom the same thing when she'd been just a girl... his baby girl, Jumper missed her with every fiber of his being. It had been a blessing when Sera had come out looking so much like her, and the older she got the more she resembled Chandra. He glanced over at Ashton with a quizzical look on his face. "What was Wayne here for Ash?"

Ashton was getting a little tired of answering the same question, it was enough that Sera seemed to be suspicious but when his granddad started keeping a keen eye on him he felt like a bug under a microscope. Shrugging he rubbed his palms on either side of his jeans and crossed his arms in the same defensive pose Sera had adopted earlier. "Nothing... Clarice called him... about dad, she seems to think there's something strange about his death, so Wayne came out to check on it. I think she needs to be let go. She's getting too nosy for her own good." The way he said that almost sounded like a threat and he grimaced slightly in realization. "I... I just mean with what we are and all, I don't think we should have human help here at the farm." Some of the tension in the air seemed to leak out, but the hole was nothing more than a pinprick at best.

Jumper seemed to be giving the idea some thought and slowly nodded. "I think you're right Ash, I'll have a talk with her... let her know we won't be needin' her services anymore." He glanced at Sera and as though sensing she needed it, he walked over and placed an arm around her pulling her close. "You feel like helping your old granddad pluck some feather's girl?" Ashton took the moment of reprieve he'd been granted to exit the kitchen, he was in need of a shower after working on the farm all day. His intention was to get the hell out of the house tonight, off the farm, away from the speculating and almost accusing eyes that seemed to be watching him every moment. It was time for one of his all night excursions, it was long overdue.

CHAPTER SEVEN
(MISSY & JUNO)

She lay there semi-conscious, her head was pounding and she groaned inwardly as a sharp pain sliced through her stomach. She felt nauseous and knew she was about to toss her cookies on the rug beside her bed if she didn't move quick. Lifting a hand to her forehead she was surprised when the touch felt sticky, tacky as though she'd had her fingertips in a bucket of Karo syrup. She opened her eyes slowly and looked at the tips of her fingers. They were red, bright red with a little bit of crusty brown where the blood had begun to dry. She sat up so fast she almost cried out as fresh waves of pain and dizziness assailed her. What the hell had happened last night? Looking down she realized that the entire front of her t-shirt and jeans were covered in blood. Her sheets looked as though they had been soaked in it and for the first time in years Missy began to panic.

Had her mom seen? Had she come in? Surely not she would have woken her up screaming and demanding to know what she'd done. The only option she had was to move fast before her mother woke and came into her room. She jumped up from the bed, this time ignoring as best she could, the pain behind her eyes and vertigo that almost caused her to fall forward. Beginning to strip off her clothing she wadded them up and started ripping the sheets off her bed. Bits and pieces of her memory started to come back to her as she worked and the horror she felt mixed with a feeling of fear so profound washed over her almost causing her to hyperventilate.

They'd killed someone... something? A lot of something's... cows, five of them. Mr. Macy's farm... oh shit she was in so much trouble. He had camera's they'd be caught. JUNO! It was his fault, the bastard! He'd made her do it. There'd been a bottle of Vodka and another of Everclear under the seat in his brother's truck and they'd had some kind of party in the bed of the truck, smoking cigarettes, laughing, and talking. There were holes in her memory, some the size of a pinhead, others the size of golf balls. She could only remember snatches of what they'd done and could barely remember just how they'd slaughtered the cows. Tossing the ball of clothing into her adjoining bathroom she placed both hands to her head as tears spilled down her cheeks. She could suddenly remember the screaming of dying cattle and... she'd laughed... they'd laughed as though it was a huge joke. The sadism in which she'd committed such an atrocious thing appalled her and she couldn't understand what had come over her to be able to do something so horrible.

She had to get to school, but first she had to get rid of any evidence. Some of the blood had soaked through to her mattress, quietly she went out to the kitchen, still in her bra and panties and came back with the bleach and an old towel. She began to work feverishly at scrubbing the blood off the mattress in an effort to at least lighten the stain. She could always pretend it had been an accident, she'd started her period in the middle of the night... she hadn't known... when she was done she went into the bathroom and showered, that was where she broke down. Tears streamed down her cheeks and soon she was in a ball on the shower floor. It was the sound of the door closing that got her up and moving. She cut off the water, toweled dry quick and stepped out. Grabbing an old quilt she tossed it over the lightened stain on the mattress just as her mother opened the door. "Missy, you're going to be late." She stood there framed by the first rays of sunlight from the living room window down the hall, her hair stood on end, and her eyes were glazed with the after effects of whatever she'd shot up with the night before. "I know... I'm almost ready." She glanced toward the bathroom door and prayed her mother wouldn't come further into the room. "Well... hurry up, you're walking today too, I don't feel like drivin' ya. I'm going back to bed." She turned then and headed back into her room shutting the door firmly behind her.

Missy breathed a sigh of relief and hurried to get dressed sliding on a new pair of jeans and another t-shirt, these were about all her wardrobe consisted of. Looking around she found an abandoned Wal-Mart bag from a recent purchase and stuffed the bloodied clothes and bed linen into it. Burn the evidence... it was almost as if someone had spoken the words to her and she instantly searched around for her Zippo. She found it on the bedside table and with bag in hand started out into the backyard. While the clothes and sheets burned she stood there almost numb. She had to find Juno... she didn't know what she'd do, but she had to find him... she had to know why. Making sure the flames were extinguished she buried the evidence, digging a hole with a shovel from the shed and making sure the ashes were well covered just in case... sliding her Zippo into her jacket pocket, she stuffed both hands in after and started the trek to school.

Juno was an oil spill. Once unleashed, everything he touched was forever altered. He was waiting for Missy at her locker, leaning against the cool metal in a pose of casual indifference. His t-shirt was brand new and still had that crisp quality about it. His jeans were worn impossibly low on his lean hips and each time he moved, whether to fold his arms or cross one ankle over the other, they appeared to be in imminent danger of falling off completely. His designer boots were crafted from imported black leather. It was his favorite color. Hell, it was his favorite expression. 'The color of his soul', he liked to joke. The same shade of his hair. "Amata mea." He said the greeting that was becoming familiar between them since the night before. Despite his presence at her side, Missy's classmates continued to pass her by without a glance. Juno preferred it this way, having her all to himself. Missy just wanted a little attention, and with Juno, that was what she got. Since they had met, he had aligned all of his interests to her.

He moved closer and reached for her. "Let's get out of here." He suggested in that honey-rich, deeply penetrating voice. He had a way of speaking that cut off her attempt at vocabulary. When she opened her mouth to speak, his was already moving. The same could be said about their bodies, as well. When she stirred, he was there, pressing his frame angled toward her, tugging her away from any direction not of his choosing. "I have a few bottles in my truck." He continued as the soles of his boots shuffled silently across the tiled floor, herding Missy in the direction she'd just come. The bell rang and the crowd began to disperse, still Juno's interest remained honed on Missy, as if there was nothing more important than her submission. There wasn't, he silently conceded, grinning down at her. "I know a place," He said, sliding his finger through one of the belt loops in her jeans, "where we can go," his opposite hand moved to her waist, before he lowered his head, "if you want to be alone?" The words were warm against her skin, with just a hint of whiskey mingling on his breath.

She'd tried, she'd entered the building catching sight of him at her locker and even though he looked like a God standing there she had every intention of railing in on him about the way she'd woken up this morning. Even as she now walked with him toward the double doors to exit the way she'd come in, she still could not figure out what it was that had stopped her words from spewing forth with every vile thought she'd harbored. The moment she'd stepped in front of him she'd felt it, a kind of vacuum that seemed to pull her in and close behind her. It was almost as if she'd stepped into a bubble that had been delicately sliced only to close up again and no one or nothing else existed but Juno and her. Glancing up at him she watched his jaw tighten as they exited the building, her gaze shifted and she looked back a little surprised that no one seemed to be watching them at all. She felt his hand twist at her side as his finger looped into her jeans causing her to suck in a breath successfully cutting off her ability to even think.

They were at his truck before she could make words exit her lips, though every dialogue she'd practiced on the walk to school seemed lost. Only one quick thought seemed to make it's way past the world she was now encompassed in... Juno's world and that thought was just how furious her mother would be if she skipped school again. "What happened last night?" It was the only phrase she could muster and as he opened the passenger door she slid in waiting for him. She jumped slightly as he closed the door behind her and dropping her bag to the floor she wrapped both arms protectively across her chest. Unnatural... the word rang through her head as she watched him walk around the front of the truck and though she knew it wasn't right she wanted him more than she'd ever wanted anyone or anything in her entire life. He was malice tempered with lust, horror laced with beauty, death... smothered in androgyny... and she found that she wanted to die when she was with him. He had a cigarette perched between his lips when he climbed into the driver's seat beside her. Casting a quick glance toward her, Juno leaned forward, and grunting, shoved his hand under the seat. Empty bottles rattled across the floorboard, knocked carelessly aside as he searched for the whiskey.

"You want to know what happened last night baby?" He asked, whispering the endearment as he scooted across the cab like a prowling feline. Juno liked keeping proximity with Missy. He liked to feel the warmth of her flesh, enjoyed how her pulse raced when he brushed against her. He thought it was amusing, how she tried so hard to please him. Even now, he could smell distress

44

on her. It wafted from her flesh like a fragrant perfume. "You lost a little... control." He said, closing his fingers over the cool bottleneck. "But I was there for you, Amata mea." The whiskey jostled as he sat the bottle on her lap. "I'll always be there for you." Straightening, Juno kept his gaze firmly fixed on Missy, reading every expression that filtered across her face. His features remained impassive, as though chiseled from stone. Sliding the key into the ignition, Juno arched his hips from the cracked leather seat before retrieving a Zippo from his back pocket.

"We were going to have a little fun right?" He asked, flicking the lighter cap back and lighting a new cigarette. Staring out of the windshield, Juno inhaled two thoughtful drags before continuing. "But as soon as you took the knife, something happened to you. You wouldn't talk to me. You wouldn't listen." He dropped his head and raked both hands through his blue-black hair, before glancing toward her once more. Although his expression hadn't changed since they first climbed into the cab, Juno's voice thickened, and each word was heavy with anxiety and excitement. "You were free, Missy. Fuck, it was beautiful! I stood, and I watched, amazed by how fucking gorgeous you were. How sexy. How mature. Everything I've ever wanted." The more gruesome details were glossed over in favor of recapping how stirring her performance had been for him. With the engine idling, Juno exhaled a slow, decadent cloud of smoke between them. "And when you were done, you asked me to help you. And I did, it's what we do Missy. Me and you... we help each other."

She'd been shivering the entire time he spoke, and even though she wanted to deny his words she had no power to do so. Her arms were still crossed over her chest and she wondered how she could be so cold. Oddly enough it seemed his words melted the ice that had formed around her little by little until she was so warm she wanted nothing more than to tear her clothes from her body... maybe even her skin. She was hot now, and though she kept her head angled toward the floorboard she cut her eyes secretly to steal a glance. The blood... it didn't matter anymore. The screams of the cows... they slowly began to silence themselves. The horror of remembering how she'd been the one to wield the blade... she found it exhilarating. Her memory started to come back in slivers and she turned fully to face him. "Me... and you..." She worshipped him... it was wrong, and she knew it but she didn't care. A smile started to form and she moved to straddle him, mindless of the steering wheel pressing against her back.

A savagery overtook her and she began to kiss him, hard and though she could taste brimstone and ash on his lips, it only excited her more. This was what hell tasted like... she'd thought it would be scary, and had been terrified of it all her life... it really wasn't that bad. "Atrum angelus..." She didn't know where the words came from she was unaccustomed to speaking anything but English but they formed on her tongue without thought as she parted her lips from his. Dark Angel, she knew that was what it meant... had he put it there? What else could he do? She ground her hips against him and could feel the noticeable difference in the looseness of his pants. Virgin or not she wanted him inside her... needed him to fill her up completely. She should have been scared, in fact Missy should have been terrified and if she'd have been sane she'd have leapt from the truck and ran as fast and as far away as she could... but in that moment she'd lost all control, she was his now.

His hands were brutal as they gripped her, guiding her body closer to his, forcing her flesh to reform beneath his touch. There was a ferocity radiating from his being, threatening to burn the skin from his bones. Hunger clawed from the pit of his stomach, transforming him into a beast right before her eyes. Snarling, Juno roughly jerked her from his lap and shoved her back on the seat. With a speed that seemed unnatural, he had positioned himself between her skinny thighs, and was lowering his mouth to taste her once more when a heavy bang interrupted the chorus of their heavy breathing.

"All right, knock it off in there."

Juno went perfectly still, but remained hovering above Missy. His features contorted in a mask of pure, unadulterated rage. When he didn't immediately respond to the cop peering into the window, she firmly rapped the end of her flashlight against the door again. Dropping his head forward, Juno inhaled deeply. "We weren't doing anything." He said, before tossing a hard glance over his shoulder.

"It sure looks like you were doing something to me." Jacy replied with a pointed glance at the whiskey bottle on the dashboard. "Let me see your insurance, registration, and license." She strained to look around him as he slowly straightened with a curse. "Missy, is that you?" Jacy was familiar with Missy and her mother, having been called to their home on more than one drunken occasion.

"Look, lady-" Juno began, digging his wallet out of his back pocket.

"Let me stop you right there. I'm not interested. License, insurance and registration." She replied in a clipped tone.

Gritting his teeth, Juno silently forked over the items she demanded, before leaning toward the floorboard to collect his discarded pack of Marlboros. Flipping the top back, he plucked a cigarette from the box, and winked at Missy as he offered her the pack. He didn't have time to even thumb his lighter before Jacy cleared her throat.

"Okay, asshole. Get out of the truck." She even opened the door for him, after she tossed his papers onto the dash.

Juno threw his head back and laughed so hard his shoulders shook from the effort. The grin on his face was wider now than it had been seconds ago, when he'd offered that reassuring gesture to Missy. "You're going to arrest me?" Juno narrowed his eyes on Jacy, considering the severity of her threat, as he lit the cigarette still perched between his chapped lips and slowly inhaled.

"I'm not going to ask again. Missy, stay in your seat." Jacy reached for the holster of her gun, and snapped the security latch that held it in place.

"For fuck's sake." Juno cursed, stretching his neck until he was rewarded with the satisfying sound of a pop. "It's okay, baby." He reached for Missy and slid a hand beneath her hair, cupping her neck. It took another threat from Jacy for Juno to break his eyes away from Missy's, it was as if he had been searching for something in her gaze, had been feeding from the strength in her soul.

This couldn't be happening, she'd been ready, more than ready and even though his quick moves had frightened her a little she felt the excitement deep in her core. The wrap on the window made her jump and she watched the altercation between Juno and the cop almost in a trance. When Jacy called her name she barely registered who it was and rewarded the officer with a meek smile. She could tell Juno was pissed but she could barely register anything beyond that as though he'd taken something from her... a part of her soul or essence. Feeling his hand beneath her hair, resting warm and slightly moist against her neck she only nodded as he spoke.

Waiting for a chance to break in as she saw things becoming more serious she spoke up. "It's ok... Jac... I mean officer Crittenden... we were just talking... really." Then her gaze caught the bottle on the dash and she gave Jacy a withering look. "That's not... I mean this is his brother's truck... that's not ours." Her entire body started to shake as she thought about what her mother would say. Of course it was alright for that bitch to do whatever she wanted but if Missy so much as smoked a cigarette in her presence she was called a whore and low-life.

Sighing she settled down in the seat feeling a little like a child being scolded and realizing that Juno was less than happy with her for having even spoken a word. What was his deal? There was something about him that was starting to scare her, it was almost like a spell was beginning to lift and she was remembering where she was and exactly what was going on. Had she blacked out? No... she remembered what they'd been about to do and realized at that moment that the button on her jeans was undone. She quickly reached beneath her shirt to snap it back together only to realize that Jacy was staring hard at her.

As he climbed out of the truck, Juno cut a glance toward Jacy's belt, and noticed that her hand had moved away from the gun and was now reaching for her handcuffs. Without being told, he turned around and put his hands behind his back. He stomped one boot and then the other, straightening the leg of his jeans. No matter how hard he tried to catch Missy's gaze, she avoided his eyes. He could tell by her body language, along with her determination not to glance in his direction that she was panicked.

"Hey," He said in a calm, reassuring voice that sounded nothing like him. "It's okay, baby. Remember? Me and you." Even after Jacy had snapped those cuffs onto his wrists, he was trying to catch her eyes. Hauled into the back of the police cruiser, Juno silently stewed, unable to do more than watch as Jacy returned to the truck.

"Look, I don't want to call your mom." Jacy said, leaning into the truck to address Missy. After visiting Missy's home, as many times as she had, she understood that in most situations, the young girl wasn't the problem. She seemed like a decent kid, she'd just been dealt a losing hand. "But you have to promise me that I'm not going to find you in a position like this again." She gestured to the whiskey bottle and cigarettes with a jerk of her chin. "If I do, there won't be any calling your mom. You'll be in that backseat, too. Do you understand?" Though the question was firm, that same hard edge did not reach her eyes. Missy reminded her so much of her own sister, at that painful age of discovery. Jacy didn't think there was enough money in the world to get her to return to those awkward, agonizing days of her youth.

Missy finally looked at Jacy but not long enough to hold her gaze. Panicked wasn't the word she'd have used at the moment. Scared to hell and back... more like it. As Jacy spoke she nodded her head and breathed an audible sigh of relief. "Thank you... but..." She was about to ask if she could let Juno go but decided against it. She had already pushed her luck about as far as it could go. In the end she decided less was more.

"I promise... you won't catch me in a position like this again." She wasn't about to promise she wouldn't end up in a position like that again, just that she wouldn't be caught. Glancing back through the rear window of the truck she saw Juno sitting silently in the back seat of the cruiser. She knew she'd see him again soon, there was no way in hell they'd be able to hold him for long. His brother would get him out, Jesse would do anything for Juno. Their relationship was a bit odd. She climbed out of the truck and shoved her hands in the pockets of her jeans as she headed back across the road to the school. She only glanced back once more and saw Juno mouth something to her, "Amata mea", swearing she could hear what he said she nodded and smiled, then moved on disappearing back inside the school.

CHAPTER EIGHT
(MIDWAY HIGH SCHOOL)

Jacy watched until Missy was inside the building, she witnessed the slight pause as she glanced back and could have sworn she saw her head nod in the direction of the back seat of the police cruiser, but when she turned back to have a look, Juno was staring straight ahead with no indication of having made a motion in Missy's direction.

She decided to let Juno sit there a bit longer, she wanted to have a talk with him, a serious one. Jacy walked back to the driver's side of the cruiser and opened the door taking a seat. At first, she purposely avoided looking in the rearview mirror as she grabbed her trusty notebook and began writing a short description of Juno in case it was needed later. "How do you know Missy?" Her voice was sullen and she kept the tone even, yet clipped putting on her best impression of 'the deputy.' Finally finished writing, she glanced up into the rearview mirror and scanned his Juno's expression as he spoke.

"Her mom and my brother... have this... thing." He smirked, a slightly lopsided grin, those piercing blue eyes stared right back at her without any sign of blinking. This guy had a way of making her feel as though she needed a hot shower. It wasn't hard to tell that he had a way of injecting emotions into a person's mind, almost like a giant mosquito with a projectile entering straight into your brain.

"What was your brother's name again? A... Jesse, I believe?"

He nodded slowly, his eyes still trained on her reflection. "Yup, that's him. But if you're planning on calling him, he's not in town."

"Not in town? Where would he be if he's not in town and you have his truck?" Already the answers to her questions were getting interesting and she hadn't made up her mind if she intended to take him to the station or not.

"Right... well he used the car. See we do have two vehicles. I don't much care for walking to school, so he lent me his truck and he took the car. He's in Charlotte." His expression suddenly became guarded as though he was hiding something.

Jacy dropped her eyes for a moment, no longer able to handle the odd, niggling feeling at the base of her skull. "I see." She had finally decided she didn't want to spend any more time with him than she had to. Keeping her eyes down, pretending to dig around in the seat for his paperwork which was actually lying neatly on the dash of the cruiser where she'd tossed it earlier, she spoke again. "Listen... Juno, I don't know what your intentions are with Missy, but regardless of her mother's extra-curricular activities she's a good girl. She has a chance to be better than that." She glanced up finally and grabbed the registration and his license from the dash handing them back to him over her shoulder. "I'm going to tell you this in a language you can understand." Her eyes stayed on his no matter how hard she wanted to divert them. "Don't fuck her up.... you got it?"

"Oh, I don't intend to... I have nothing but the very best of intentions Ms...?" There was a slight hardness to his expression as he spoke and Jacy had to resist the urge to tremble. What the hell was with this kid, he was no more than seventeen at most but it seemed his soul was much older.

"Crittenden.... Deputy Crittenden." She didn't like the way he'd looked at her at all and she slid from her seat, glad she'd left her door open, walked to the back door of the cruiser and opened it. She grabbed his elbow and hauled him back out, turned him around quickly and began to undo the cuffs. "You had better do right by that girl, she deserves better. My advice to you would be to go in there and tell her at the first break that it's over. I don't know you Juno... but I don't have to know you, to know that I don't like you." She pushed him forward slightly and hooked the cuffs back on her belt stowing the key.

"Oh, I don't think I'll do that, but I will take good care of her deputy. Don't worry your pretty little head about that." As she looked up at him she fought the urge to slap his smug face but legally she couldn't put hands on him just as she had no reason to take him to the station. There was nothing left to say, nothing she could say so she turned and got into her car. She didn't care if he went back inside or not, she just wanted to get as far away from him as she could.

Juno stayed outside and watched her leave, tracing the path of the car with his eyes until the dust settled and she was gone. Yup, this town was going to be fun. He'd been to quite a few hotbeds of excitement in his life but none like this. He'd make good on his promise to take care of Missy, but he was almost sure that his idea and Deputy Crittenden's was far from the same.

CHAPTER NINE
(THE POLICE STATION)

"**W**ell, I met an interesting character today..." Jacy tossed her keys up on her desk and they clattered loudly shifting papers in their wake. "Do you know a... Juno Reed?" She finally glanced over at Wayne and noticed he was sitting with his head down almost between his legs, hanging over his desk-side trash bin, which was no small feat for a man that had a belly the size of a beer keg. "What's wrong Wayne... one too many of the Red Dog's chili burgers?" She smirked, and a short laugh escaped her, but the look was quickly replaced with concern as Wayne suddenly tossed his cookies slightly missing the trash bin, splattering quite a bit of bile on his shoes. When he was done he looked up, a supremely agitated glare in his bloodshot eyes. "Shut the hell up Crittenden!"

"Holy shit... what happened to you?" She moved over to his desk and propped herself with one hip on the edge. "Sorry... but you look like shit."

"Trust me... I feel like shit, and don't mention anything to have to do with..." He heaved and turned his head just in time to let go another bout of bile. He had meant to say the word 'cows' but it never passed his lips. What he'd seen at the Macy's farm today had him seriously contemplating ever eating another piece of beef ever again. He finally righted himself and leaned back in his chair. "We'll discuss my day later... when I can keep myself from hacking up my breakfast. To answer your question, I know a Jesse Reed... but I can't say I've ever heard of a Juno. Why, what's up?" He grabbed the cool wet paper towel he'd brought with him from the bathroom when he'd first gotten back to the station and wiped the beaded sweat from his forehead.

"Fine... but just so you know, I'm not going to forget that you owe me a story, and I fully intend to collect so you had better get your ass in gear." Jacy, smiled and continued on. "So... he says he's Jesse's brother. I caught him and Missy Sue in his brother's truck about to get hot and heavy in front of the high school this morning."

"Missy... Missy Jackson?" Wayne sat up a little taking a sudden interest.

"The one and only. Come on Wayne, how many 'Missy's' do you know in this one horse town?" Jacy shook her head and moved back a fraction as the smell of his putrid, vomit-laced breath hit her.

"Didn't know Jesse had a brother, he never mentioned it." Wayne noticed the movement and held his hand up to his mouth in an off-attempt to keep the scent back. He wasn't too concerned as he knew he'd never have a chance with a woman like Jacy, but still it was damned embarrassing.

"That's odd, he did say he was his brother." She slid off the desk and stood again, starting to pace in front of his desk in thought. "I'll have to check up on that. So... you ready to tell me about this day you had?"

Wayne shook his head, the visions coming back in garish detail. He felt like his stomach was pretty much empty by now so he nodded. "Yeah... I think I can manage it. God... it was so damned horrible."

Jacy's right brow raised, she hadn't seen Wayne like this in... well... never. "You went on that call this morning... the one a the Macy farm right?"

"Yeah... that's the one. Damn Jacy, I wish I'd have let you take that call." He had started to look a little green around the gills again but he went on. "Damn cows... everywhere, blood everywhere. It was horrible. Their throats had been ripped out, stomachs opened and intestines..." Well, he had thought his stomach was empty, before he could finish the last word he was hanging his head over the trash bin again. Finally, he was able to bring himself around and sat up taking a deep breath. "Jacy, I've never seen anything like it. I don't know if it was an animal or what but what I don't understand is why it would wrap the intestines around the neck of each of the other cows... there were five of them, each one's intestines wrapped around the neck of the other in a makeshift noose. The majority of their organs missing, it was sick. I can't imagine an animal doing that, it was almost like something from a horror movie where they sacrifice things... sick." He dry heaved again but seemed to have control on keeping the bile from rising finally.

Jacy had seen much worse having come from New York, she wasn't too much taken aback by the description but it was still bad for a small town like Sampson County, and this right on the heels of the Morris patriarch's death. Could there be a pattern? Perhaps the elder Morris' death wasn't as cut and dried, as it seemed. Jacy always had a way of trying to tie things together but that was just her training at work. She'd dealt with more than one serial killer type murder in her time. She still didn't understand why she had jumped at the chance to take a position here, other than the fact that she needed the break. It seemed like that break wasn't about to come anytime soon. "No, definitely not an animal from what you're describing." She was thinking hard on this one now, and had she chanced a look at Wayne she'd have been surprised, his face currently registered alarm.

"Well, it's my case, I'll handle it..." He meant his words to be the nail of finality but he could tell he should have kept his mouth shut. Jacy was a determined woman and she would be sure and keep a sharp eye on him from here on out. There were things Wayne knew about in this town that was better for Jacy not to know, at least until he could ease her into it gently. "Likely some kids playing a prank, though how they had the stomach for it I couldn't say... but you'd be surprised at some of the things they get into around here. I told old man Macy I'd follow up on it and look into a few suspects I have in mind."

Jacy knew he wanted her to let it go but she couldn't help but ask, "So... you mean to tell me you have kids around here that would be that vindictive?" Her face was one of acute disbelief as she watched him squirm in his seat.

"Yeah... sure... you've seen the movie '*Carrie*' right? That one... by... that guy, *Stephen King*?" He wiped his palm over his face and down his neck, he was starting to sweat again, this time though it was from her questioning and not the sickness he'd battled earlier. "Happens now and then, especially around this time of year; close to spring and all, they get a bit crazy. Seen some real crazy shit but... well... nothing like this really. Most of the kids 'round here know how much the livestock mean to the farmers, can't believe any of them would be so bad as to take down five cows like that. What's even crazier is the fact that after the first... the other cows apparently didn't run. Usually one whiff of blood and they go insane trying to get away, even if it's not their own."

Shaking her head she moved to her desk, she needed to jot a few things down about her run-in today and would make a few notes on Wayne's case as well without him knowing. She needed to go by the Reed house later and see if she could speak to Jesse. "Sick bastards if so... they had better hope I don't catch their asses doing shit like that. You don't harm innocents... human or animal." She scribbled vehemently, almost as if she intended to scourge the town of the horrors by a simple stroke of her pen.

Wayne calmed down a bit, thinking he'd dodged the bullet for the time being, but he was sure that bullet was a heat seeker and it would come right back around eventually.

CHAPTER TEN
(THE MORRIS FARM)

Sera's birthday dinner the night before had gone off without a hitch even though the youngest Morris sibling was still mourning her father's death. That morning had been quiet and it seemed the worst was over. Sera had received a new iPhone and several other gifts the Morris family had pulled their funds together to buy her. They lived a comfortable life, but not one that allowed for overabundance and it had taken them over a month after her birthday to save up for it all. Ashton was reminiscing about the joy on her face, a happiness he'd not seen since their father's death as he sat upon the old rickety tractor in the north field on their land. It would soon be time to plant the next crop and he was turning the earth to get it ready; this year they intended to try their hand at cotton in that particular area in the hope that the money would be much more than they'd had the year before with the corn. He suddenly noticed Jumper's truck barreling up the pathway and with a grinding of gears, brought the tractor to a halt. Jumper never drove fast, with the way he was headed up to the field, dust flying in his wake, there had to be something wrong.

The tractor quieted almost at the same time Jumper's old truck stopped next to it and he sprang from the cab with a purpose. His face registered lines of anxiety that was near panic. "Where were you last night Ash?" This conversation was long overdue and Jumper was ready to get into the thick of it right then and there.

Ash jumped down from the tractor and ran his right hand through his hair. "I was here, at home. I didn't go anywhere last night, why? Is something wrong?"

"The Macy's lost five cows last night." His words almost sounded like an accusation and Ash swayed a little on his feet as if his grandfather had struck him.

"And you think I did it? Jesus, pop, you can't possibly think I'd do something like that." Ash was astounded and shook his head as he spoke. "It wasn't me..."

Jumper moved in closer and placed a hand on Ash's shoulder. "Son... you need to tell me what happened. I can understand you not telling your sister but I need to know for my own sake. Your daddy's dead son, and I know you killed him that much is clear, but Ash... I need to know why or it's going to be damn near impossible for the family to move forward."

For the first time Ashton had tears in his eyes and he lifted his right hand to place it atop Jumper's as they stood in silence for a moment. His grandfather's hands were rough and callused like his own, but there were lines of age that had crept in recently and he could feel each one as his hand rested atop Jumper's. He finally roused from his momentary state of what seemed like meditation and spoke. "I had to, what I'm about to tell you may seem crazy or even damn near impossible but, I didn't know how to say it or how to make you believe me. I guess now I'm going to have to just come out with it and hope for the best." He glanced down to the dark soil beneath their feet as though he hoped it would swallow him up, but there was no hope of that happening anytime soon. Looking up and straight into his grandfather's faded blue eyes he pulled the lid off the pot and let the contents of what was hidden there spill to the ground.

"Mom's alive pop and she didn't run off with another man, she was taken and freely given by my father." The words uttered from Ashton's mouth made Jumper sway, his hand left Ash's shoulder, the only thing giving him stability and he dropped to the ground. "She can't be Ash... David said..."

He was cut off quick as Ash knelt beside him. "I know it sounds insane pop... but, I promise you I'm not lying. Dad is responsible for what happened to her. He didn't know I was listening when he took a call in his room that night. I heard everything. As much as I hated to lower myself to Clarice's level I didn't have a choice. I heard him say something about if they kept her longer he wanted more money. He said her name pop, he said mom's name. If she wasn't alive then why would he be talking about someone keeping her longer?" Ash dropped to the ground to sit beside Jumper. "I went downstairs and grabbed the other phone. I was careful not to let him hear me and I heard the rest of the conversation. This man was talking about mom and how they needed more time to do the tests and he couldn't let her go until they were through. Then I heard dad mention his gambling debts and how he needed more money to cover everything or else he'd have to sale the farm. I panicked after that and put the receiver back slowly so if he heard a click he'd think it was just static, but not before I heard the man say the name of some place in Raleigh, I think that's where she is, Carolina Biological Supply. It wasn't long after that he came downstairs, I pretended I was hungry and looking for something in the fridge, he leaned around the door and said he was heading out for a bit. I didn't wait after the front door slammed. I snuck out the back and shifted, and then I followed him. I was so damned angry; I don't think I've ever been so angry in my life. After he'd entered the woods at the back of the house I went after him. I attacked before he could change, I know it was a cowardly thing to do but I couldn't help it. Once he had realized what happened he shifted and we fought for at least an hour or more. I finally got a good grip on his throat and ended it. That bastard sold mom... he sold her to pay his fucking debt and told us she'd ran off because he knew he'd never get her back. He doesn't even care about her pop, he never did, he didn't care about the pack, he sold her to some goddamned science lab. So yeah, I killed him and I'm sorry but I don't have any remorse pop... none."

Ashton went silent and Jumper was so shook up by what he'd just heard he couldn't breathe. His eyes flooded with tears and he leaned over grabbing Ash and pulled him in tight. He wrapped his arms around his grandson and both of them broke down. He whispered in Ashton's ear, "We'll get her back son... somehow we'll get her back. I knew your mother wouldn't have left you and Sera like that. Chandra is a strong woman, and she loves you both so much." His voice cracked with the weight of his grief and he finally let Ash go and leaned back. "We have other things to deal with now. We have to get our house in order before we form a plan to go after your momma son. The Macy's cows... they were killed ritualistic-like. I heard Wayne talking about it to that purdy deputy lady at the café over in Spivey's Corner today. I won't repeat what was done to them, but I didn't truly believe it could have been you or any of us that did it. We eat what we kill, when we have to kill and we have our own supply of meat right here. This was something else Ash, something evil. We need to clean it up quick, I want you to get closer to that lady deputy, see what you can find out. We need to stop this before it spreads."

Ash nodded and wiped the tears from his eyes with the back of his hand. "Yeah, I know... do you think they'll kill her at that place?"

Jumper shook his head and stood up brushing both hands on his jeans and offered Ash a hand. When he'd pulled him from the ground he spoke. "No, I don't think they will, you said you heard something about blood and testing, they apparently know what she is and they're trying to do something with her blood, they need her too bad and as much as I hate leaving my baby girl in that place, we can't go get her and bring her home until we make it clean here again."

Ash knew what that meant, for years they'd been the guardians of Sampson County, they'd kept a vigil over the place and had done a good job of keeping evil at bay, but something dark had crept up on them as though they'd been asleep and it would not be ignored. "This place, those damned ley lines. It calls 'em almost like holding out a bone to a dog." Ash couldn't help but chuckle a little at the analogy. "We'll get it done... and then we'll go find mom. I'll go out to the Red Dog tonight, maybe she'll be there. She's young, I'm sure she likes to drink when she's off, maybe I'll get lucky."

Jumper nodded. "Just don't get too lucky... you know what I mean boy."

"Yes sir." He gave his grandpa another hug and a hearty clap on the back before turning to head back to the tractor. "I got to finish this field and I don't have much daylight left. It'll be time to plant that cotton before long."

Jumper stood back for a moment watching his grandson and realized in that moment just what a remarkable young man he'd become. It was his turn now. David had never been a true pack leader; Jumper knew it from the moment their families had converged for the good of the pack and the hope of more offspring. David and Chandra had been the only ones to conceive and did so twice. They were lucky, Chandra's sister, Samantha had married a man from a remote pack in the mountains and the fact they'd never been able to have offspring was because of a taint in the bloodline and he was sure it was on Tobias' side. Jumper's side of the family had always been as fertile as rabbits. Samantha was too old now to conceive. It would be time soon to try and introduce Ashton to another pack and he already knew which one it would be. The Kasa's from Cherokee were depleted down to only three members and they were looking for a fresh start. Emily Kasa, her dad Robert and a brother, Douglas around Sera's age were perfect. The father was too old and had passed leadership to Emily, she stood as Alpha now and if he could make a match with her and Ash and perhaps get Sera interested in Douglas they could make a go of it and perhaps the bloodlines would be pure enough that Ash and Sera, when she was out of school and of age, could bring some new life into the pack. All that would come once the land was purged of this lurking darkness. It was time to send the demon back to hell and move forward toward the betterment of the pack. Jumper had a feeling that it might get worse before it got better.

CHAPTER ELEVEN
(MISSY & JUNO)

Jumper would be right; more right than he'd even know. It was that night that Juno decided to call on Missy again. He'd made sure that her momma would be busy he had a very special evening planned for the two of them. Juno had styled his black hair, his eyes a piercing blue just added to the air of insanity and allure that surrounded him. If Missy hadn't noticed she'd notice tonight that his pupils were always dilated to the point that it seemed they would cover the iris completely, but just enough color showed as to give him the look of a sinister playboy.

Walking up to the screen door he jangled a set of keys in his right hand, he was wearing black slacks and a white shirt that was open at the collar, the relaxed swagger made him all the more irresistible which was what he was counting on. Tonight he'd seal the deal with Missy and make her truly his, his puppet for all the world to see. This was his favorite part, when he'd take her body and soul and consume every ounce of her to the point where he could practically tell her to bark in public and she'd do it just to please him. He truly loved this. Being a Ukobach was one of the most amazing things in the world. Chaos demons were the ones that humans needed to watch out for most. They loved the deranged, the ones that were on the verge of a psychotic break, they enjoyed dysfunction an chaotic lifestyles, they fed on fear, loathing, envy, gluttony, want and sex. Sex was Juno's favorite and he knew how to do it so well. This was how he planned to seduce Missy and make her his once and for all.

He knocked on the door knowing she was home, her mom was out tonight and the house was quiet. They could finish what they'd started in his brother's truck earlier that day. His fingers tingled just imagining the feel of her skin beneath them, he was becoming excited just by the simple thought and he knocked again to be sure she'd know he was here.

It wasn't long before Missy came to the front door, he loved the way she looked. Her eyes showed the vulnerability he so craved she was so close to a psychotic break it wouldn't take any time at all and she'd give in completely to his every will. He had plans for her, grandiose as they were he wouldn't reveal them, he'd see them played out in full detail and let the chips fall where they may.

"Well hello there beautiful, can I come in?" He actually asked permission this time, he wanted this night to be perfect to be one of the best nights she'd ever had in her entire life. She pushed open the door showing him that quirky little smile he enjoyed so much, the smile that showed the crazy lurking just behind it and as he slithered by her he made a point to brush his shoulder against her nipples. He could already tell they were hard. If he could get that reaction just by showing up then he knew the rest of the night was going to be delicious.

He had been carrying a long-stemmed rose in his right hand and just then handed it over to her, she started to go put it in water and he stopped her telling her they'd be needing it soon. There was no patience in his tone, he was ready and he wanted her now. Grabbing her hand he laced his fingers in hers and led her to the bedroom. She had yet to speak a single word other than about putting the rose in water.

Missy was on fire, her entire body felt hot and she thought she might have a fever. His presence was enough to cloud her judgment and make her long for him with such acute passion as to feel like knives carving her insides to mush. She swore just the motion of her legs as she followed him to her room would cause her to orgasm and she let out a small whimper as the thought came so very close to fruition.

"What's wrong baby?" As they entered her room he pulled her close and held her body tight against his. She sighed longingly and looked into his eyes. "I can't wait.... I wanted to but I can't." Her voice quavered with such intensity and the closeness of him made it harder still for her to hold back her desire.

"You don't have to.... I'm here, you're here and no one is going to stop us. I don't care if this whole damned place falls down around us, when I have you I won't let you go until I'm good and ready."

Missy could hardly think of anything to say the only words to slip from her lips were those of want and need. "Take me... please take me now."

Juno loved to play and so he'd start slow, urging her to lift her arms to rid her of her shirt and bra he began to trace a finger around the soft mounds of flesh and finally to the nipple where he tugged hard once then lightly caressed each one first with his fingers and then with his tongue. He suckled there and let one hand slip between her legs, even through her jeans he could feel the heat of her and the wetness, so wet he thought she may have urinated a little. He pressed hard and then lightly his other hand coming to rest at the button of her jeans as he undid them and pulled them down over her hips. She wasn't wearing underwear, all the better for him to have quick access. He had forgotten that she was still holding the rose, before he'd go further bringing her to complete satisfaction he took the rose from her left hand and brought it between them. He plucked one petal and told her to eat it as he plucked another and did the same. He then brought the prickly stem to his chest and pierced the skin with the thorn. A long stream of blood ebbed and he then did the same to Missy bringing the thorn down between her breasts. He bade her to drink from him and she did, his blood was like a mixture of soot and fire. She was sure what she tasted was brimstone and yet she could not get enough. So enraptured was she that Juno had to pull her away and make her stop.

He then pressed his lips to the scratch between her breasts and he felt her shiver so hard he knew she had just had the first orgasm of the night. Unable to keep from chuckling he allowed his deep voice to come forth unhindered and ran his tongue across each nipple. He began to whisper something in Latin and Missy suddenly felt groggy and weak, she was glad of the arm that snaked around her back to hold her upright. "What are you doing to me?" She whimpered again, it all felt so good but something about it also felt wrong.

"Nothing you don't want Amata mea." There it was, her pet name on his lips and she surrendered to the waves of pleasure that assailed her as he continued his litany in that impossibly low voice. He began to push her across the floor and to the bed. "Lay back for me baby." He helped her lie down upon the bed and as she spread out there he began to remove the layers of clothing that bound him from her. Soon he was just as exposed as she was and his throbbing member was displayed for her to see.

She reached for him and he obliged moving closer but just as he made it to the bed he dropped to his knees and took her thighs pushing them open a bit more, before she could even gather conscious thought he buried his head there and began to clean the area from her earlier spill. She wanted to scream but part of her was still worried that her mother may come in at any moment and hear. She began to cum violently and it seemed it was back to back, she couldn't stop. Her body began to convulse with each new sensation and she writhed as though possessed upon her bed. She didn't even realize when his right hand lifted and ran the entire thorned stem of the rose down her stomach, making a trail of blood that he immediately abandoned his former post to lap up as though supping from a holy vessel.

She felt a pressure and a mild ripping and he was suddenly inside her. She immediately came again and this time she didn't care who heard. She screamed and continued to move erratically. Soon her rhythm matched his and she wrapped both legs around him just as his head came down again to clean the fresh blood from between her breasts. He was her master, the one she would always be bound to and she'd never leave him.... and something told her he'd never leave her.

She came so many times she lost count, he was a master at the technique and just as she realized her body could take no more he released inside her, spilling his seed into the confines of her wet womb. This night secured his longevity as well as his station with her. She'd be his forever now and nothing would ever part them. It was at that moment that Missy's mother did, indeed come back home. She shouted out and Missy froze. She was still on the bed naked but when she leaned up ready to tell Juno he'd have to hide, he was already gone. He was like smoke or wind, he had disappeared along with his clothing. Missy's mother came into her room and looked at her. "Slut." She spoke under her breath as she noticed the bedroom window open with curtains billowing in the slight breeze. "Who is it? If you're pregnant you may as well find another place to live... I'll not have it... or you under my roof." With that she turned and went into her room not even worried that it could have been an intruder.

Missy balled up on the bed and began to cry. Suddenly she stopped as she thought she heard a voice from deep inside. *"Kill the bitch."* Missy stood up, went into the kitchen and got the biggest butcher knife she could find. Turning she went back down the hall to her mother's room and opened the door, the knife glinted in the moonlight and she smiled as she saw the shock and horror in her mother's face. "I'm so fucking tired of you, I hate you, you are the reason my life is shit and it's time for something new. I will bathe your in blood tonight you horrible bitch." She ran toward the bed and jumped high landing flat-footed on the bed over her mother. The first strike with the knife landed squarely into her mother's temple, the others landed in various places. Juno watched from the window with a malicious smile on his face. So it wasn't the poetic murder he'd thought it would be but boy was it bloody and well deserved, that was one soul collected for his master and more to come. He laughed silently as he watched the horror play out and indeed Missy did bathe in her mother's blood and it only served to start the growth of the seed he'd planted inside of her.

CHAPTER TWELVE
(GETTING RID OF THE BODY)

It was safe to say that Missy, the sweet, even-tempered young girl was gone and a woman now stood in her place. This woman however, was nothing like the child she had been. There was a new knowledge a keen conceptual mind lurking beneath her own and it told her everything she needed to do to take care of the mess she'd left in her mother's bedroom. No one need know about 'her', she didn't even exist as far as Missy was concerned. In fact, if she had it her way she'd be forgotten about very soon.

Missy had taken the keys to her mother's old 1968 Chevelle and drove to the local hardware store. Mr. Dodson was there and a bit surprised to see Missy as she entered. "Well now, did you get your license then?" He'd never known Missy to drive before and he was in shock to see her in his store on a Saturday. She kept her tone clipped, short and sweet. "No time for chatter old man, I need lime... you got any?" This was indeed very different from the norm. Missy had never been so angry, so mean.

"Yes... yes of course it's in the back against the wall there. You may need some help lifting it... one bag... two?" Dodson watched her odd behavior.

"I got it, no need to stress yourself." She went straight back to the wall, grabbed one bag, hefted it on her shoulder and came back to the register and asked how much. She'd taken her mother's purse and pulled out a crisp twenty dollar bill.

"You only need one?" He would almost wish he hadn't asked at the look she gave him. He was still having trouble believing that she'd lifted an entire fifty pound bag of lime all by herself. "Three dollars and twenty-five cents."

"Fine... thanks keep the change." She tossed the twenty at him and headed to the car depositing the lime in the back seat before heading to the driver's side, getting in and practically leaving tracks as she tore back down the road toward home.

Once there she got out and hefted the back onto her shoulder again. She barely seemed to notice the weight of it as she went up the few wooden steps into the trailer. She went down the hall and to her mother's room, she wasn't worried about getting rid of the body all at once, it could sit for a while and slowly rot away. It was the smell she wanted to hide the most. She kicked the door the rest of the way open with her foot and moved inside, not even bothering to clean up the blood she sat the bag down on the floor, opened it up, hefted it again and began to pour the lime over her mother's gaunt corpse. She could lock the door and simply pretend her mother was sleeping if anyone came by. No one gave two shits about that bitch anyway especially not Missy.

CHAPTER THIRTEEN
(RED DOG SALOON)

Ashton was antsy, it had been a while since he'd gone out and now that he'd spoken to Jumper he was feeling a lot better about the future and his position in the pack. All he needed now was a night to cut loose and have some fun, play a few games of pool and drink a few beers. He was also half hoping he'd run across that deputy lady, wasn't her name Crittenden? Something... Crittenden. Well if he did run across her he'd better figure out her first name fast or he'd look like a complete and total ass if he didn't and actually tried to talk to her.

Ashton wasn't much of a fixer upper. He didn't waste time on his hair or his look. Straight out of the shower he pulled on a pair of Levi's, a plaid Wrangler shirt and his boots that he used on the farm. He combed back his long sandy gold hair that made him look a little like a lion on the prowl and he was out the door in less than fifteen minutes.

By the time he got to the Red Dog he was ready for a good night. He was hoping the lady deputy was here. Jumper had told him to get close and he planned to do just that. How close he got would depend on her. His main obstacle here was to find out what the hell was going on in his town. Yes, it was his town the sheriff's department be damned. The Morris family had and always would watch over Sampson County it was their world and he'd be damned if he'd let anything happen here that he didn't know about and couldn't fix.

As he climbed out of the old beaten up Chevy truck his boots made a grinding sound on the gravel beneath his feet. He thought he heard someone call his name and turned in time to see Tonya Renee, his favorite bartender, come bouncing up to him.

"Well look at you handsome, I haven't seen you here in a month of Sunday's." She laughed and wrapped both arms around his neck giving him a big smooch on the cheek. Tonya had to struggle to reach that high, she was all of five foot and weighed about a hundred pounds soaking wet. She was forty five, with auburn hair and dark brown eyes. A beautiful woman and she had the biggest crush on Jumper even though he was a good ten years her senior.

"Where's my main man tonight?" Those brown eyes held a hint of sparkle as she spoke of Jumper and Ashton had to hold in a chuckle.

"He stayed at home darlin' he was a bit busy when I left him. Seems some woman he's seeing now..." His words drifted off as Tonya gave him a light punch in the gut.

"Woman my ass, he better not be seein' no other woman but me. You tell him I said that too." She laughed again and hooked her arm into his. "You best be behavin' tonight too, you know he has me watchin' you when you're here and if you get into any mischief I wouldn't be surprised as big as you are if he didn't still tan your hide good."

Ashton had to laugh at the mental image. Yet he would bet there would be a tussle between the two were he to get into something he should avoid. "You ain't got to worry about me none Tonya, you know better."

"I know, I know... come on then, let's get you a drink, first one's on me." She released him as he opened the door for her to walk in ahead and even though they never charged him a dime he still paid his five dollar cover and followed Tonya to the bar. He sat down on one of the stools and waited for his customary Budweiser.

It was all of less than an hour before he'd be rewarded with his quarry walking through the door. Damn she looked good on and off the clock. He wouldn't mind in the least getting close to Jacy, not in the least. That was all it took, just her walking through the door and he remembered her first name. "Jacy," he whispered it low in his throat liking the way it sounded on his lips. He just might have to defy old Jumper a bit and take things somewhat further if she'd allow it.

He turned back to his beer pretending not to notice her entrance and continued to guzzle. He soon called for another and had Tonya make change for a dollar so he could get in a game of pool. Always a good opener he'd ask Jacy if she played and if so that would be is opening to getting to know a bit more about the sultry black haired beauty.

He barely got to the last table at the back wall before he heard his name again and looked up to see Jacy standing before him. "Well... fancy meeting you here tough guy. You planning on another bar fight tonight or just here for a bit of relaxation?"

"Relaxation... and what about you Miss New York City, you here for a cat fight or just hanging loose off the clock?" He chuckled and pulled down another stick from the holder on the wall. Testing them out he finally found a good one and then nodded toward the rest. "Wanna play?"

"It's been a while, but I'll take you on." She too began to test the sticks till she found one that would suit and without asking she moved to the opposite end to wrack the balls. "Take it easy on me will ya?"

There was a sudden spark in his eyes as he thought of how many jokes he could have made from that one sentence and he nodded. "Easy as pie." He motioned to Tonya and she'd know to keep the drinks flowing on his tab, he had plans and he was determined before the night was over he'd get what he wanted from the deputy and perhaps a lot more.

CHAPTER FOURTEEN
(RED DOG SALOON)

The talk came easy and before long Jacy was telling Ashton all about the cows at Macy's farm and how it looked like some kind of strange ritual killing. It wasn't her case of course but it also wasn't a huge secret. By now most everyone knew about it and she saw no harm in telling Ashton what she knew. The scene had been so gruesome there was no way that most everyone for at least two counties around hadn't heard.

"We still don't have anyone of interest in the case but I'm sure we'll figure it out soon." She prepared to break the balls again and felt Ashton move in close behind her. He was feeling the alcohol now as much as she was and he placed both callused hands on either hip. Leaning down he whispered in her ear. "Might have been Wayne for all we know, you know how hungry he gets on the job."

His words caused her to almost miss her shot as she laughed so loud the other people at the table over gave her a look. "Ash... that was wrong and you know it." Still she couldn't help her laughter and just to agitate him a little she leaned her backside against his crotch. If he wanted to play she'd oblige him, she had no shame.

"That was dirty girl.... now I'm going to have to stand here a little longer until I settle down some." She'd be able to feel his slight arousal from what she'd just done and he had a feeling tonight was going to end up pretty damn good. He was still not drunk enough yet that he'd forget that one sacred rule. He definitely had to be careful sense the Lycan gene was carried through intercourse just as much as it was by a bite. He'd come prepared and though it had been a few months since his last rendezvous he'd be damned careful to wrap it up if tonight turned out anywhere near what he'd expect.

It was getting early, 'late' last call had come long ago and Tonya would be getting ready to close up soon. All night they'd been playing with one another, getting cozy and at one point their lips had been so close together he was sure she was about to kiss him but she'd backed off just in time. She was hotter than hell and he was all for a bit of mischief but suddenly as Tonya called for one last round Jacy started putting on the jacket she'd discarded earlier. "Hey, where you going?"

"You heard her, last call, that's my queue to go." Jacy shrugged her shoulders and smiled. "Don't think I didn't enjoy it though."

"Yeah, me too, I know we have to go soon, how about we go back to my place?" Ash wasn't about to let it go that easy. Surprisingly Jacy looked up shaking her head. "Oh, no... you don't get me that easy lover."

Ash cocked one eyebrow and chuckled. "And just who says that I'm trying?"

"Trust me, I know the lines the moves and everything you've done tonight has been an effort in getting something I'm not ready to give just yet Mr. Morris. But, I'll be sure and let you know when I am." With that she headed for the door but he was quicker. Determined to give her something to think about he grabbed her from behind and turned her around. The kiss he took from her was hot, steamy and laced with a promise of one hell of a good time when she did make up her mind. "Keep me notified, I don't take a snub too kindly." His voice was a deep growl against her slightly parted lips and then he released her and let her go on her way.

Ashton waited just a moment longer before he'd follow and get in his truck to head to Macy's farm. He knew the cows would be gone but he wanted to see the place for himself and do a bit of looking around. He knew he'd be able to still catch a scent and maybe if he was lucky it would lead him right to the culprit.

CHAPTER FIFTEEN
(MACY'S FARM)

Ashton drove up the short dirt road to Macy's farm and stopped the truck just short of where anyone would be able to see his headlights. He got out and crept into the edge of the tree line where he could change without observance. It hurt like hell every single time but the longer he waited to change the worse it was. He also made sure that his sister changed at least five to six times a month if for no other reason than to run the farm. He could feel every bone pop and snap under the pressure of the change and fought the urge to let out a deep howl.

He would have just walked the property but he thought better of it, he could get a better scent this way than in human form and he didn't want to get caught as himself out there just in case old man Macy heard him and decided to have a look around. He'd left his clothing behind and padded over toward the place he'd been told the cows had been laid out. Luckily Macy had already changed pastures and there were no cows in this one or else Ashton would have had it bad. He could just imagine the frightened ruckus that would have taken place and that brought on another though, why had there not been a ruckus on the night that the tragedy had happened?

He wondered if the police had thought about that or asked if old man Macy had noticed. Ashton padded up to the area where the dead cows had lain and began to traverse the spot with his nose close to the ground. By now there was a faint smell of death, blood and urine. He wrinkled his nose slightly at the nasty combination and fought his otherwise primal urge to roll in it. It took over an hour for him to catch another faint smell, one of brimstone and ash. He knew none of the parts had been burned or cooked so where did that smell come from. There was only one answer for it, there was a demon in Sampson County. He was going to find it and end this once and for all. The only thing he didn't realize is that it was already far too late. The seed that Juno had planted in Missy was ripening and it may take nine months for it to come to full fruition and then some for the babe to grow but when it did Juno/Seth would be back and there'd be worse than hell to pay.

CHAPTER SIXTEEN
(MORRIS FARM)

The Morris Farm was buzzing, everyone had a job to do and yet Ashton was paying for those few drinks he'd had at the Red Dog last night. However, he had quite a bit to tell Jumper about what he had found out about the cow fiasco at Macy's. It was an ill omen that a demon was in Sampson County, they didn't seem much of them here but when they did there was always a reason behind it. It seemed this was where they enjoyed coming to play when they had something to prove.

Little did Ash know that Jumper would have much more to reveal to him today and there was some of it that he would likely not enjoy. It hadn't taken Ashton long to realize just how much he was beginning to like Jacy Crittenden and the bad part of all that was, he'd envisioned what it would be like to have a partner that was on the police force. He was to become Alpha of the pack, and he'd need a mate that was as formidable, strong and protective as he was. He was starting to see her as the perfect prospect when Jumper suddenly tossed a monkey wrench into his plans.

They were having an afternoon break, Sera had brought out some corn muffins from the night before that she'd heated up along with some fried chicken and field peas. That girl was so much like her momma it was crazy. Not only was she the spitting image of Chandra but she had her temperament as well as her mothering attitude. When it came her turn to find a mate there was no doubt she'd end up finding the perfect one and she'd have some of the most loved pups there ever had been. She smiled at each of them and gave her grandpa a hug then turned to ash to pop him in the forehead. Before he could put is plate down to rise and chase her she was gone.

Ashton chuckled watching her sprint away and turned to Jumper. "She's just plain ole' great ain't she. I love that kid, I couldn't have had a better sister." By now everyone, including Sera knew about what had happened and plans to rescue Chandra were in progress but as Jumper had said there was a time for everything and that meant they had to take the time to plan accordingly and figure out exactly how to execute the best maneuver.

"Ash, we need to talk about the future, not your mom that's in the works but we need to get back on our feet and for you that means you need to marry and soon." Ashton turned to face his grandfather with a quizzical look on his face as though just waiting for the next shoe to drop.

"What do you mean?" The worst possible thing that could happen would be for Jumper to start getting the idea to set him up with someone and yet he had a feeling that was exactly where this was going. Ashton hadn't even gotten use to the idea of his new role in the pack yet let alone the fact that he'd have to marry.

"Jumper... come on now, this is too soon. What happened to us choosing out own mate? I thought that was the way it had been forever. What about Sera? You know she's not going to go for being forced to choose, what makes you think I will? No... no way, you can't do this to be grandpa, be reasonable now. I already have someone in mind anyway and it would be the perfect set up." Ash paused as Jumper raised his hand and shook his head.

"No Ash, if you're talking about the lady deputy you can forget that, that's not happening son. I'm telling you now we're not stepping out of bounds. There hasn't been a human made wolf in a very long time and we're not starting that now. We need strong bloodlines Ash, that means wolf with wolf, not wolf with human." He placed a hand on Ashton's shoulder and continued on. "There's a pack up in the mountains in Cherokee, they are only three now and there's one girl, she's already alpha and she'd be perfect for you. She's close enough to the same age just a year or two younger and she's beautiful, I've met her. Long black hair, green eyes and legs for days." He waggled his eyebrows and waited for Ash to respond.

"No... you honestly think that looks is all I'd care about? What about love grandpa, what about caring about someone and don't tell me that will come in time. That's what everyone says and just because she's hot don't mean that will happen. Love doesn't happen just because of looks even you know that." Ashton got up to go, he'd hear no more of this and he was pissed that his grandfather even had the audacity to think he would. Jumper called out after him.

"You have to do this son, it's the only way, she has a brother around Sera's age and her father. It would be good to have another elder in this pack besides me."

Ash shook his head and kept his pace, "Then get Sera interested in the brother... because I'm not interested period." He said it before he'd thought about it, he'd never want Sera to be forced into a marriage she'd hate and he'd be damned if he would be.

CHAPTER SEVENTEEN
(SHERIFF'S OFFICE)

"**W**ell now, look who's come dragging in with her tail between her legs this morning." Wayne was already at the office and sitting with that infamous shit-eating grin on his face. "I saw you last night girly, making time with old Ash. Trying to grab a wolf by the tail?"

"Shut the hell up Wayne, it's all work for this girl and you damn well know it. I'm still trying to find out what really happened to his old man, I still don't believe it was as simple as a heart attack. Now get up you jackass and let me sit down." She was working her thumbs into her temples, that damned headache just wouldn't go away and she regretted having had too much to drink the night before. However, there was a part of her that didn't regret all of the night before. A sly smile worked its way up her face but she was careful not to let Wayne see. "Where's the chief?"

"He's out on another call, a domestic, seems the Barbour's are at it again. Every weekend without fail they get into some kind of tiff, next thing ya know dishes are flyin' and shits hitting the fan." Wayne was glad he hadn't been called to go out there this time. The last time old Charles had come close to taking his head off with his shotgun. That mean drunk son of a bitch was nothing but trouble. "By the way, why don't you let well enough alone with Ash, he's a good boy and he don't need you digging into his vittles." Wayne raised an eyebrow in her direction and was quickly flicked off.

"Yeah, right, that's what everyone in town says but they all said the same about Dahmer too." She turned the chair around to face him. "What's the 411 on those cows from Macy's? That case closed yet or still working it?"

Just the mention of those damned cows made Wayne want to puke up his guts again. "Still working it, why, you hear something?"

"No, not really but there's this kid in town... dark sort, looks like he could be into some of that kind of shit. I think we should check him out." Jacy leaned back in the chair rubbing her temples again.

"Now let's not go making trouble where there isn't any Jacy, are you sure about this kid or is it just because you caught him messing around with Missy Sue?" Wayne slid his chair over next to her and ran into it with a light bang. Jacy kicked at him and almost landed a foot in his crotch.

"It don't have anything to do with Missy Sue, this has everything to do with my own intuition. He's bad news and I know it."

"Pfft, just like you know Ash is bad news I suppose?" Wayne covered his crotch with both hands this time, this girl was dangerous, he wasn't taking anymore chances.

"I never said Ash was bad news I said I wanted to find out more about his daddy and what really happened, I haven't put the blame on anyone yet." She said that last as though leaving it dangling like a worm on a hook.

"Well, do you know where this kid lives?"

"No, but I thought you might. His name is Juno, but I don't have a last name." She eyeballed him as though waiting for him to respond.

Wayne thought for a moment and shook his head, "Nope, never heard that name before did he mention any details like any siblings, a dad, mom?"

"No, nothing of the sort, wait, one sibling he said, a Jesse."

"Jesse? The only Jesse I know is a Jesse Newton up by Pike Way, but he don't have no siblings. He's an only child well, only son. Last I heard he was seeing Missy Sue's mom." He gave her a strange look and settled back in his seat again. "That's odd he'd say that Jesse was his brother if he's not."

"Yeah... very odd," she was beginning to think a lot of things were odd about this kid and she had an urge to talk to Ashton again. She wondered if he may know the guy or of him. Maybe that was also a way she could get closer to the eldest Morris sibling. Maybe this entire thing would be her ticket to find out the truth behind a lot of the crazy goings on here in Sampson County.

CHAPTER EIGHTEEN
(THE MORRIS FARM)

It had been a long day, there was a lot of work to be done before the harvest and Ashton was tired to the bone. Jumper had tried time and again to talk to him about the merge between the Morris and Kasa families and he'd managed to dodge him every step of the way. He wasn't even ready to be married yet was he? Still in his early twenties already saddled with the responsibility of the pack and now he was suddenly being tossed into a relationship/marriage and didn't even know the girl.

There was no way he was going to stand for it and he was even more sure that the Kasa girl likely felt the same way. They were due to be arriving within the next week and he was going to try his damndest to put a stop to the so-called merge.

He'd found out where Crittenden was staying and he had plans tonight. He was going to make a house call and see what he could find out about the issue with the cows at Macy's farm. He knew what he was looking for but he had no idea just how to find it. Sure that Jacy would know something by now he was determined to put on the charm if need be.

He showered quick, put on a fresh flannel and jeans and headed out to the local grocery for a bottle of cheap wine and flowers, at least he thought that was what you were supposed to do to charm a lady. He hadn't had a lot of practice but he'd give it a try if it got him what he needed.

It wasn't long before his beat up truck was pulling into the driveway of the newly acquired residence of Jacy Crittenden. She'd been living in a hotel for a while but finally pulled up stakes and moved into a doublewide trailer off of highway 13. It was a newer model, quite nice for a mobile home and the yard had been well manicured by the previous owners. He hopped out and headed up the drive to her front steps, she was opening the door before he even got one foot on the bottom porch step.

"I come bearing gifts, something of a housewarming. I heard you moved in out here and thought perhaps you'd be a wine drinker. I'm not much for wine so I got myself a few beers, ah... can we talk?" Ash leaned against the banister and offered her the flowers first then switched the wine off into his free hand while hanging on to his six pack with the other.

"Wine... and flowers, well Mr. Morris you do know how to win a lady over. Come on in, what is it you want to talk about?" She left him to navigate the door, which he did with ease, and she moved into the kitchen with the flowers to put them in water. "Here, give me that."

Once that chore was done, she took the wine and found her cork screw in the first drawer. Luckily she hadn't skimped on the unpacking and had it done the first day, then again she didn't have a lot to unpack. Wayne had been handy with her furniture which had been in storage for at least two months. He had put her bed together and got her all set up, tried to cop a feel when she gave him a hug and got himself smacked in the process.

"Nice place you got here." He had took the time to have a seat on the couch, that was just his way. He didn't wait to be invited to sit he just figured it was alright to do so. No sense in beating around the bush he jumped right to the real point of his visit. "The cows at Macy's, I know you and Wayne have been talking it over and I don't see much of him these days as his wife has put him in time out for bad behavior." He chuckled a little and went on. "What do you know about that whole story? Any ideas who it might have been?"

Jacy turned to look at him cocking her head slightly in curiosity. "Now why would you want to know about that and just what does it have to do with you Mr. Morris?"

"Call me Ash, please?" He said it sincerely as the whole 'Mr. Morris' thing reminded him too much of his father. "I want to know because the Macy's are friends and I want to help if I can. I don't take too kindly to someone coming into town and messing with perfectly good meat. Besides that, we trade with the Macy's sometimes meat for vegetables and those cows could have been some of ours."

"Well now, I think I can understand that but to be honest, Ash, I don't have anything yet. I did speak with

Wayne about a young man that was in town by the name of Juno. He seems a bit odd and I didn't like the looks of him. Wayne says he don't know him and that struck me odd as most everyone in this Podunk town knows everybody."

As soon as Ash heard the name his expression changed from half amused to anger. He knew that name and he knew what he was. He quickly changed his expression to one of complacency and nodded. "How old is this kid? Does he go to school?"

"From what Wayne said he doesn't even live here. He claimed he was the brother of a guy named Jesse that's been seeing Missy's mom, I'm sure you know Missy, she goes to Midway with Sera. Well, come to find out he's not this guys brother at all. So there is lie number one, then he made out like he went to Midway or at least he gave me the impression he did, lie number two. In my opinion this guy should be number one on the list of possible suspects where those cows are concerned. I didn't like the looks of him and he gave me the 'willies'. It was almost as if something was just off about him. I don't know what it was but it wasn't good." Jacy came to sit down beside Ash, by now she'd gotten a cold mug from the freezer for his beer and she had herself a glass of Duplin Red Hatteras.

"I want to help." The words were sincere and he looked her right in the eyes. "I know I'm not on the force and I know that there could be hazards but I can handle this and I really want to help. I'll go to the school tomorrow and find out what I can if you promise to let me deal with this guy and keep it off the books." Ash shifted a bit and made sure to keep eye contact. He was working the Alpha as hard as he could on Jacy even though she wasn't part of the pack. He hoped it worked.

"I don't know..." She made the mistake of looking into his eyes and everything she was saying became a huge bowl of mush. "It may be dangerous... and.." She was lost, there was nothing more to say. "Fine... but be careful and don't get in too deep, I could end up with my job on the line for this. Keep it between you and me."

"You got it." He smiled and his eyes seemed to change color, she noticed but didn't say a word the more time she spent around him the more odd she found him, but also the more she wanted to take him to her bed. Looking away she felt almost as if she'd been mentally violated, why in the hell did she give in so easily?

Ash leaned back and rested against the couch pushing his long legs out as he took a drink of beer. He knew now that she was a beer drinker too, only a beer drinker would have cold mugs in their freezer. "Do you like it here so far Jacy? I can call you Jacy right?"

She turned around and smiled, as she kept her place on the edge of the couch, it was almost as if he lived here and she was the visitor. He made her feel so vulnerable. "Sure, Jacy's fine. Why don't you tell me about yourself Ash, by the way, I'm sorry about your daddy..."

He stopped her before the words could get out and said, "Don't be, trust me, if you knew him you wouldn't care that he was gone." He couldn't half believe he'd said that and instantly felt as though he shouldn't have. "He was just a tough man to like is all." He thought that may keep her from asking anymore questions, he knew that was where this was headed.

He was fast to turn it all around. "Tell me about you, I'm just an old farmer just like any other around here. We till the land, farm it, drive tractors and old pick-up trucks. There's really nothing more to tell." There was so much more to tell but he couldn't tell, and he knew that. There was no way that a girl like Jacy would ever understand his true nature and the way things really were. If she knew what she was dealing with, with those cows she'd likely have a heart attack. Juno was a Ukobach, a lower level demon and if he was hanging around Missy she was sure in some serious trouble. Ash just hoped he could put this one back into the ground before it was too late. Little did he know that it was far from too late already.

"Well, I was born and here I am, basically I went into the force because my father was in and I carried on his dream. I have a little sister back home that I plan to bring here before too long so I decided to leave her with momma until I had a place and the money to care for her properly. She's about the same age as your sister Sera, how is she by the way?"

"She's doing good and I'm sure she'd love to meet your sister once she's here. Sera's a good kid, she keeps her nose right in line where it should be, she's a hard worker and extremely bright for her age. She's also very mature. I'll be sure and bring her around when your sister gets here." Ash shifted again, he purposely allowed his hand to brush her thigh and slid to the edge of the couch level with her. "What's your story anyway, all that at the Red Dog the other night...."

"What do you mean? I was just following the leader darling." She slid closer to him and grabbed his hand putting it on her thigh, "There are a lot of things that we can keep secret Ash... lot's of things, if you're hurtin' just tell me and I can make it go away."

He squeezed her thigh and then moved his hand away. "I'm hurtin' alright but that's not why I came tonight and I'm unprepared darlin'" He made the motion of wrapping it up and laughed. "No offense to you of course but I like to keep things neat and clean."

She almost wanted to smack him, was he indicating... surely not. Only Ash knew what he'd meant by what he'd said and it was indeed best for her that he have protection handy else she'd end up with something far worse than a simple STD.

He stood suddenly and brushed his palms down his jeans. "How about I make you a promise to take you up on that Suarez another time, perhaps when we're both ready and not just jumping into things? I plan to see much more of you Jacy... a lot more." He came closer and grabbed her face in his hands planting a kiss to her lips. He allowed his hands to roam over her body and he truly liked what he felt.

He released her and backed away. "I gotta go, but I'll be back another night, tomorrow maybe? Once I find out more about this Juno character?"

"Sure, by all means the door is always open for you Mr. Morris." She smiled knowing he'd take the hint.

CHAPTER NINETEEN
(MISSY & JUNO)

Kimberely Pennin was a very pretty blonde, cheesy cheerleader type that took her pride in winning ribbons riding horses for show. She never missed an opportunity to thump Missy in the back of the head as they traveled in opposite directions down the crowded hallways. She was your typical show-off, the kind of girl that was popular with the rest of her ilk but was secretly hated by most of them. She was always handed everything on a silver platter though she was hateful, snotty and thought she deserved the world and then some.

She saw most of the girls that tacked her horse as only fit to lick her boots and treated them just as badly as she did Missy. That particular day, Missy had had enough and she told Juno after school about how badly she wanted to get back at the bitch for all the shit she did to her. She not only abused Missy but made sure to bully her on a daily basis calling her a whore like her mother as well as making vulgar hand gestures inciting some of the boys to do the same. Embarrassment was the order of the day for Missy and the new power she seemed to have now that she was carrying Juno's seed was intoxicating enough that she no longer gave a shit who she hurt, how badly, or even how it was done.

Missy never seemed to find it odd how no one else could not see Juno when she was with him while they walked down the hall together at times between classes. She realized that some of the kids seemed to look at her oddly but she wasn't sure why. She just continued to carry on her conversation with him as they went out the door and got into his brother's truck. "I want her dead, not just hurt Juno, I want her dead! That bitch has had it coming for a long time and I'm not going to take her shit anymore." Missy had lit up a cigarette as she spoke and took a long drag. She was dressed very unlike herself having taken to her momma's closet lately. It was a good thing there was no stench in there since she'd used the lime to cover everything before. Her mother was rotting quite nicely by now and Missy found that she actually enjoyed checking on the progress daily... like some seriously fucked up, macabre science project.

"Where's she going to be today 'Amata mea'?" Hell, he was game, he didn't really care what she wanted, she could have anything at all. He just loved the chaos and especially murdering spoiled bitches, that was his style. He shifted the truck into low gear and started to slow down a bit just in case he needed to turn off soon.

"I heard her tell her friend Danielle that she'd be going to ride her horse today at the stables she frequents and how pissed she was that no one would be there to saddle her horse for her. She'll have to do the dirty work herself it seems. Can we go?" She looked at him hopefully with baleful blue eyes knowing he'd give in. Just one more thing she loved about him, he'd give HER anything she wanted and Missy had never had that before. Though what she wanted more than anything in the world was revenge, sweet undisclosed revenge.

They'd already been heading in the right direction and she suddenly told him to slow a bit more. She could never find the driveway to this damned place. She finally spotted it and told him to turn in slow. It was just around 6:00 PM an she knew that Kimberely would be just finishing up for the day. They pulled up slowly and she had Juno park just in front of the barn. Sure enough Kimberely was still out riding on her dark bay mare; content to sit and watch for a bit Missy whispered, "Fall bitch... fall..." It was at that precise moment when the horse suddenly spooked and raised up on her hind legs. A seasoned rider Kimberely seemed to hold her own for a moment until the animal began to buck uncontrollably. The bucks weren't just your normal crow hop but serious bucks of anger and the normally sweet natured bay gave some hellish sounding snorts to go with them. It only took a moment or two before she felt her neck snap sharply and couldn't feel her legs, she came off and landed hard on one of the t-posts that made up the fencing area as it pierced her shoulder she let out a fierce cry of pain.

Missy was laughing, cackling uncontrollably, then she saw the blood and couldn't help herself, she got out of the truck and headed over to where Kimberely was lying barely conscious unable to get her arm off the post as she'd slid all the way down, it was a good thing that the wire had not been live. "Well... looks like you need some help shall I call 911?" Missy was enjoying the hell out of this, more than she likely should have. All Kimberely could do was nod slightly as her neck was killing her. "No... I think not, oh Juno? Be a doll and come help me with Kimberely here." That's when she'd finally see him, the one Missy always talked to in the halls, the reason everyone said she was crazy, it had to be a trick, just a fevered mind in pain, there was no way he was really there. He looked like a dream, beautiful like an angel with the smile of the devil himself.

"No... no please..." it was at that moment that Kimberely knew she wouldn't make it through the night. She had heard rumors, how everyone thought Missy's mom was dead because she hadn't shown up to work in days. Now she realized, almost as if she could see the entire thing play out behind Missy's eyes that her mother was indeed dead and it had been by Missy's hand. Kimberely began to cry as Juno bent to pick her up under her arms and pulled her painfully from the t-post that impaled her. As he moved her upward he bent his head slightly and at an odd angle to lick the drops of blood from the cold iron.

Kimberely screamed as her shoulder tore from the socket as she was lifted from the pole. They'd have fun with her tonight. The bay mare had quieted down, Belle was her name. Missy rubbed her right hand down her jeans and back up taking a switchblade from her pocket. The horse had seen too much, at least that was what her fevered brain told her. She headed for Bella and there was a loud screech from the animal as Missy took the reins and plunged the switchblade into her throat.

The horse reared once and dropped as Missy moved back, the thick blood draining from her jugular.

By this time Juno had poor Kimberely in the truck and was waiting for Missy, they were both lucky that there were woods on either side and no one had seen tonight's insanity at CKF Boarding Facility.

Once Missy was in the passenger seat she leaned over to Kimberely and looked at the wound in her shoulder shaking her head. "You poor little thing... that looks like it hurts pretty bad." She stuck her finger in the hole pressing hard and ask Kimberely screamed she laughed sticking the finger in her mouth. "How yummy..." Still laughing she watched out the windshield as she asked Juno, "So where we taking her?"

"I figured your place, put her in with your mom." Kimberely, having heard this began to try and fight but to no avail. Missy punched her in the wound and she became a mewling baby once more. "No now none of that sweet thang. My place sounds just fine, I can see how long it takes for that pretty face to melt once we're done with her."

They soon pulled up into Missy's drive and easily carried Kimberely in. She'd given up fighting after everything that had happened she'd lost a lot of blood and knew she'd be dead soon. As she awaited her fate she began to go back over her life and all she'd done and a part of her supposed she deserved this. Once she was placed on the kitchen table and tied down she'd live just long enough to see what she looked like from the inside before her vision faded and she was gone.

CHAPTER TWENTY
(THE MORRIS FARM)

"Hey Sera," Ash was headed down the stairs into the kitchen as Sera was in there doing the dishes. They'd just had a pretty big supper which every night was a pretty big supper in such a large family. Everyone ate at the main house and that meant enough food to feed an army. It was a good thing since they'd lost Clarice that they had his aunts to help with the cooking. They'd both given up their day jobs, which weren't really needed, to help Sera around the house. After this last fiasco with the death of David, they had decided it best to keep things more solid and close knit keeping outsiders out of their business.

Jumper and Ashton had retired to the living room earlier to talk about the merge that Ash was still highly against. There were soft tones laced with anger and loud tones laced with family affection but still a hardheadedness that was largely due to both men not able to see the other's reasoning. They were bound to quarrel it was just their way. It finally had ended with Ash leaving to go to his room only to now enter the kitchen to address Sera. "Do you know a guy in your school by the name of Juno?" Sera stopped scrubbing the pan she was in the midst of to turn and face him. By now she had found out about their dad and still was angry with her brother even though she tried hard not to show it. There had to have been a better way to handle things than to simply get into a knock down, drag out fight that had ended in his death. "No... not unless you're talking about Missy's imaginary friend." That immediately struck a mental chord with Ash though he didn't let it show. "Imaginary friend?"

"Yeah, everyone in school is talking about it. She's always walking around mumbling to herself and sometimes just speaking right out loud to someone named Juno that no one can see. I think her mom has finally knocked her for a loop one too many times. It seems she's truly lost it finally."

"That is odd." Ash shook his head and pretended that he understood what she meant and knew what she was talking about even though he really knew the truth behind it all. It was just as he had expected, Sera wasn't old enough to study everything there was to know about the occult and that book would be revealed to her late but he knew and had guessed as much that this Juno was indeed a Ukobach, a lower class demon that was hell bent on making his master happy and would only appear to a person or people when he felt it was needed.

He decided to quickly change the subject, "You have band tomorrow right? Am I coming to pick you up or is

Jumper going to get you?" He also needed to know so he could have a chance to speak with deputy Crittenden again and try and talk her out of this crazy demon chase that she had no idea she'd gotten herself into. This was dangerous, much too dangerous for her to handle.

"You're supposed to get me." She turned again to glare at him as though she wished Jumper was coming instead of Ash, she was not ready to approach the subject of why their father had to die, she still knew nothing about their mother, Chandra being locked up in Raleigh in that damned institution and Ash and Jumper still hadn't figured out how they were going to get her out.

"I'll have grandpa come get you I have something else I need to do." He hadn't figured out just how to break the news to her about their mother being alive so he was avoiding those awkward moments alone with her as much as he could as well.

"Fine..." This was all she'd say before drying her hands and heading up to her room passing him in the doorway with not so much as a backward glance. He longed for the day they could mend the rift between them right now and knew it would come but he still had no idea just how or when.

CHAPTER TWENTY-ONE
(THE MISSING GIRL/POLICE STATION)

School was all abuzz the next day when Sera got there people were saying that Kimberely Pennin was missing and nobody knew where she was. There were jokes being made by the kids that never took anything seriously that her horse and her had simply run off but none of them knew the details that the police did. Her horse had been found with its throat slit in the arena at CKF Farms and there had been blood on a t-post that had turned out to be that of the missing girl but they couldn't find her anywhere.

Missy just continued to talk to Juno as they traversed the halls not mentioning a thing but thinking the entire post insanity was funny as hell. You'd have thought she was someone famous the way some groups talked about her, others actually acted as though they were glad she was gone. Most people didn't seem to care either way and weren't at all concerned. High school was funny that way, the different clichés were always interesting to watch. It was truly odd watching Missy with her right arm looped into someone else's that was not there as far as the classmates were concerned. She'd have made the perfect mime at a street fair as she made it all look so very real. They were sure she was crazy, even the teachers gave her a wide birth when they saw her coming.

Back at Missy's place poor Kimberely had joined her mother on the bed, lime laced and looking like a gluttonous cannibal with her intestines stuffed in her mouth. It had been a beautiful picture and anyone that got hold of Missy's phone could have seen the amazing selfies she'd taken if they only cared. But for now she'd get away with her gruesome deeds and continue on with her insane bloodbath there would be at least one more murder before this chapter of her life came to a close.

Kevin Sharp was the ultimate jock, not captain of the football team but very close and today he'd think it a good idea to play a joke on Missy. Little did he know that the joke would be on him. He had left a note in her locker to meet him after school down by Cape Fear River at the basin area right off Highway 13. This would be the only body that Missy would not take back to her home and it would be the beginning of her undoing.

She had no idea that deputy Crittenden had been following her since Kimberely had been reported missing she had a feeling she'd need to. So when she saw Missy and Juno come out of the school at the end of the day she began to creep along at a good pace so as not to let them know she was following. The problem came when they went off road down the path that led to the spot Missy was to meet Kevin she lost them for at least an hour and by the time she made it to the place for the rendezvous it was far too late. What she saw caused her to reel backward in horror.

There was a tree that had long been dead, the boys head was wedged into the 'v' of two branches, his entrails were in Missy's hands as she laced them in and out between the branches and Juno was no where to be seen. Not understanding what exactly was going on and worried about her own safety, she immediately called for backup and Wayne headed her way while she stayed in the woods unable to do anything but stare at the macabre sight.

Once Wayne got there they moved in, arresting Missy was easy even though she screamed and fought calling for Juno the entire time; she wasn't that strong, and they could not understand how she could have overpowered Kevin alone and done this to him. They got her into the backseat of the cruiser and called for EMS to come out and collect the body of the dead boy. Phone calls would have to be made to the parents and there would be a witch hunt, there was no doubt. Now it was their job to keep Missy safe until they had all the details. Police procedure followed they soon left with Missy and headed back to the police office to question her. All she would say was Juno did it... over and over again. There was no doubt the girl was mad as she told them in detail about the other murders and where to find the bodies of her mother and Kimberely Pennin.

There was a sad look on Wayne's face, what no one knew was that this could possibly be his little girl here about to spend the rest of her life in an insane asylum because of a boy that by all counts and purposes didn't even exist.

CHAPTER TWENTY-TWO
(JACY'S HOUSE)

Ash had heard everything on the news. Sampson County didn't make the news a lot unless it was about the local Hollerin' Contest or someone's meth lab had blown up. He immediately got into his truck and headed over to Jacy's house. His first thought was to make sure she was alright and his second was to find out the details that had been left out by the local news. Sera was distraught, she hadn't been friends with either of the kids that had been murdered but she was still upset by it simply because you just didn't expect things like that to happen at such a young age. Even though she was a shifter, there were just some things you couldn't wrap your head around and one of them was the fact of just how horrible some humans could be to one another.

He finally made it there a little past nine that night and taking the steps to her door two at a time he was soon knocking loudly. "Jacy, it's Ash, open up, I need to talk to you about Missy." He waited for her to answer the door and when she did what he saw took him totally by surprise. She looked shell-shocked, her hair was a mess and her gaze was vacant as though she were in shock, he couldn't help himself, he immediately grabbed her in his arms and hugged her tight. "Oh no... I'm so sorry, we need to talk and I have a lot to tell you, things you won't believe but you need to know."

He released her and allowed her to move back so he could enter. After she was back inside and the door was closed he looked at her for a moment and waited for her to speak. "Ash... it was horrible, I've never seen anything like it my entire time on the force including in New York. There was so much blood and she was happy about it, it was as if she reveled in the fact that she had murdered him. How can anyone be that crazy Ash? I don't get it."

He nodded slowly and moved to take a seat on the couch motioning for her to come sit beside him. "Jacy, the things I'm going to tell you tonight... I don't want you to get upset or think that I'm crazy too. But that wasn't all Missy that you saw there, remember that guy you told me about, Juno? He's not what you think he is, he's not human Jacy, he's a demon, a Ukobach, a lower level demon that has basically come here to play and I'm sure he's not done yet."

She looked at him still with a slightly vacant expression. "I don't want to hear this... I can't hear this right now Ash, please..."

"No Jacy you have to hear it and you have to believe, look I don't want to do anything to scare you but if I have to I'll show you the truth about me just so you will believed what I'm telling you. You can't work here in this town without knowing and I don't know how the hell Wayne thought that you could. The reason Wayne didn't bring me in for questioning about my father's death is because he knows what we are. Wayne knows that we aren't just human beings Jacy. My family... me... we're shifters, we come from an ancient race of people that date back to the BC time period. I swear to you I'm not lying. I know you've asked questions before and I know you still want the truth about my father.... the truth is... I killed him. I had to. I found out that he had sold my mother to an institute in Raleigh and I murdered him because of what he did. He couldn't run the pack, he'd have sold us all out just for the money, he's never cared about the pack or any of his kin." There it was, he'd just laid it out on the table and he prayed she'd see reason and believe him.

"No... no no no no, things like that don't happen Ash, I think you need to leave." She stood up and backed away, her eyes were wild now and Ash didn't know what else to do. First he looked around to be sure her firearm wasn't anywhere near and as he stood he removed his shirt, he wouldn't change fully, just enough to prove to her that what he was saying was the truth.

"Look... I don't want you to freak out and please don't get your gun and shoot me I'm not going to hurt you. I'd never hurt you Jacy, but I need to show you so you'll believe me." It hurt like hell, his bones began to pop out of their original location and regroup into new areas, his skin tightened and rippled. Hair began to sprout from his chest and face. His mouth and nose reformed themselves into a gaping maw and he tried to speak but couldn't form words. His eyes turned a brighter green and he reached out to her with sharp fingernails that was once a normal hand.

Jacy freaked, she screamed but instead of going for her gun she fell back into the kitchen and balled up into the fetal position. Ash noticed this and immediately changed back allowing himself to relax. The reverse was much easier than the initial change and he immediately moved into the kitchen to where she was. "Jacy... it's ok... it's me, Ash, I'm not going to hurt you." She still stayed away and only looked up at him to see that he'd indeed changed back to the human he was. "I'm so sorry, it's the only way I knew to get you to believe me."

It was too much in one day, she couldn't believe what she'd just seen and after seeing what she had before with Missy, she just couldn't comprehend it all. "Leave... please just go... let me think. I need to think."

He understood, she needed time to understand it all and he'd give her that. "It's ok... I know... I'm leaving." He moved back and was careful not to touch her. He'd wait for her to come to him when she was ready but right now he needed to find that demon and get rid of him somehow.

CHAPTER TWENTY-THREE
(LOOKING FOR A DEMON)

As promised, Ash left Jacy's house and began his search immediately. The first place he went was Missy's home to see if he could find Juno there. The place had been cleared out and he had to go beneath a lot of crime scene tape to get inside but when he finally did, there was nothing and no one there.

His next stop was at Jesse Autry's house. He banged on the door only for it to be opened by Jesse's father. When he asked where Jesse was he was told that he'd not seen him in several weeks. He wondered why the father hadn't reported the disappearance but when he asked he was told that Jesse often disappeared for days at a time and he'd not suspected any fowl play. Chances were that Jesse may be among the dead and no one had found his body yet. Ash didn't say a word, he simply thanked the man and moved on to every place he could think of where a lower level demon would hide. Every single place he went to turned up nothing, he couldn't even find Jesse's truck.

True to his thoughts once he'd given up the search, the very next day they found Jesse's truck with Jesse in it. He'd been disemboweled much like the other victims of Missy and Juno's this meant that Jacy was still searching too even after Ash had shown her that the world she now lived in was not the world she thought it had always been. There were monsters and not all of

117

them were human. Jesse's body was badly decomposed and anyone could tell that it had been moved from where he'd met his end and placed in the truck as though a final goodbye to the people of Sampson County. There was no way they were going to find Juno. These demons were shifty and smart they could be anyone they wanted to be and they could change into anything they wanted at any time. The fact was, Juno was not done playing yet, he receded back into the hellish darkness that he'd come from only to await that special gift he'd left with Missy.

EPILOGUE
(THE ASYLUM)

Jacy finally calmed down enough and realized that her reality was not the same as it once had been. She had thought about leaving and had even packed up a lot of her things over the weeks after the mess they'd cleaned up here in Sampson County. There was a lot still needed to be done by way of paperwork but just when she thought she couldn't handle it there was that voice in the back of her head that told her no matter where she went there were still things out there that she would never fully understand. It was much easier to handle them in a small town than it would be a huge city.

Missy had been taken to the local asylum and placed in a padded room. She had taken to harming herself after she realized that Juno was gone and no one wanted to lose her... least of all her father, Wayne. There had been a DNA test and he knew now that Missy was indeed his biological daughter. His wife left him taking the other kids with her. He was going to have a very rough time of it and even though he'd see is other children from time to time, he knew that Missy and the grandchild she was carrying would always been his priority.

The seed that Juno had left behind... that was going to be quite an interesting child. Missy spent most of her time cradling her growing stomach and rocking slowly back and forth as she sung lullabies to the baby that grew within her womb. There was so much that the doctors wanted to learn about her and from her she'd never truly give them much, but enough so that they could try and understand the horror and the havoc she had unleashed upon the people of Sampson County. There were many parents that hugged their children close, so glad they had not become part of her killing spree.

No one ever saw Juno again and likely never would. He'd already moved on. Likely to the next town but then again... he'd had so much fun in this one and there was so much more to be explored, would he ever truly be gone?

Ash had gone back to his quiet existence and awaited the Kasa's move to his farm. They'd be there in another year or so and in the meantime he still argued the case with Jumper. He wasn't ready for the responsibility of a family, he had way too much left to do, the top of his list was to get his mother out of that damned facility in Raleigh. Chandra would come home, this he vowed to the entire pack. Luckily, Jacy had calmed down enough to allow Ash back into her life. They saw one another on occasion and became quite close. No one knew of their secret get togethers and Ash made sure to keep it a secret especially from the pack. He was sure that Jumper and the rest would not approve of him making time with a human.

Sera finally got over her grief and was able to put on a brave face around school. Still in the back of her mind she could not fathom why Missy had done what she'd done and Ash never did hand out details to anyone other than Jacy. Time would pass and things would get easier the town would settle down and life would go on. But no one knew what was just around the bend there were many more monsters clamoring their way up from the abyss and a town where ley line intersected calling their name that was ripe for the picking.

ABOUT THE AUTHOR

Morrigan Austin is the single mother of an amazing daughter. She is a writer, an entrepreneur, a singer and an animal and human rights activist.

She sometimes writes under the pseudonym Kitty 'de Chatfou her book next book is due out later next year 2019, and will be her third published work.